JOE COGGIANO

Taking Back Tomorrow

First edition

This book was professionally typeset on Reedsy.
Find out more at reedsy.com

To Cara

All the adversity I've had in my life, all my troubles and obstacles, have strengthened me… You may not realize it when it happens, but a kick in the teeth may be the best thing in the world for you.

WALT DISNEY

Contents

Acknowledgement

Acknowledgments

Special thanks.

To the editors who helped me make this readable. Brooke, Brian, and Ryan, I hope that you're as proud of the finished product as I am.

To Mike Dio for the cover work.
  www.diotattoos.com

To Sean and Aj for all the technical support and consulting that helped shape the story.
  To all my friends and family whose words of encouragement kept me on track and made me finish, you have my gratitude.

1

ONE

June 1

Joe loaded up heavier than usual for the trip out. He wasn't sold on the plan, but if things were going to remain somewhat safe where his family was, he would have to start pushing the problem away from his parents' farm. That meant going to a place where a lot of people he didn't know had a lot of guns.

Joe sat his body armor in the back seat of the old F-250 pickup, next to the Benelli M4, and a case of buckshot. He made sure the mags for his AR-10 and Glock 21 pistol were full, then checked the blades on his knives.

"This is boot camp shit," said Joe's brother Ryan from the passenger side of the truck. "Why the fuck do I have to check these load outs?"

Joe let his younger brother vent because he knew by the way his temples pulsed from underneath his standard marine haircut that he would need another minute before he could be reasoned with. Once Ryan's shoulders finally relaxed beneath the form fitted shirt, Joe had his window to reason with him.

Joe said, "Because—shit! Edge of the woods, two Zs." Ryan dropped the gear and caught up to Joe as they raced across shin-high grass in the front yard. Joe drew his pistol telling Ryan, "Take the right, I got left!"

The Zs raced toward Joe and Ryan, closer and closer, and when they got within ten yards Ryan shouted, "Now!" The pistol fire cut through the eerie

1

quiet that felt all too common these days. Ryan's pistol shots hit center mass, while Joe's shots hit the zombie in the shoulder and stomach. Ryan's target faltered and started to fall, while Joe's had slowed, but was still advancing. Joe aimed the pistol again as he heard the shot fire from the second story window of the old gray farmhouse.

Joe's cousin Alex had shot from a 30-06 hunting rifle, causing the remaining zombie to collapse a few feet from Joe.

Joe learned early on that traditional zombie stereotypes didn't apply. These real-world zombies could bleed and die.

When the zombie fell, Joe glanced at it before walking away. As Joe neared the truck, Ryan shouted, "Shit, Joe. It's Jeff. Jeff Reynolds."

Still looking out at the field, Joe said, "It's why I had such a hard time shooting him. I'd hoped he had made it out of town when I hadn't heard from him." He sighed and stared at Ryan. "Let's go. We'll give him a proper burial later."

Joe looked at Alex still standing in the farmhouse window and said, "Thanks, cousin."

When Joe and Ryan reached the truck, Ryan's face narrowed. "Guess I get to play gunny then. Where's Rachael?"

"I bring Rachael, then Cara has to come. And this isn't the time. Come on, we're running late." Joe turned, spotting Alex and Spencer rushing toward the truck from the farmhouse.

Both men were tall, though the similarities ended there. Spencer used to have the build of an interior lineman, but this new world had trimmed him down, and now he looked more like an undersized tight end. Alex was solidly built, but wiry, less thick than Spencer. Alex was Joe's cousin and the two looked so much alike, they had often been mistaken for brothers—even twins on occasion.

Joe nodded. "Rock and roll."

The four of them loaded into Joe's truck and headed out. Joe's stepfather, Greg stood on the small deck out front of the farmhouse. He waved and tried to smile as the truck pulled onto the road, heading across the street into the small suburban neighborhood. Greg had pushed to join them, but

Joe insisted he stay and watch the farm.

The first stop was Tim Seaford's parents' house. A few miles away from the farm, it was a small brick rancher that backed up to the park. Tim and his brother Christian sat waiting in their truck, fully armed. Tim smiled, tapped the AR-10 in the gun rack, and said, "Nice day for a hunt!"

Tim was one of the only people Joe knew who actually looked younger today than he did before the outbreak, but even his youthful grin couldn't hide his anxiety. Tim stood about 5'8" and 215 pounds and had two sleeves of tattoos, while his taller, older brother Christian stood at 5'11" and weighed in at 230 without a single bit of ink.

The next stop was Dell's house on Main Street. As they pulled up to the blue two-story house, they found him cleaning a few geese at the top of his driveway. Dell Bauer was a commercial fisherman. He and Joe had spent countless hours on the water. Dell, who might have weighed 165 pounds soaking wet, was the only member of the team without a military background, though he had more time behind a hunting rifle than anyone Joe knew.

"Got you guys a couple of birds this morning," Dell said as he stood and walked to Joe's truck. "Man! Where ya'll headed? Doesn't look like the usual hunting trip."

Joe smiled. "We got a meeting with some people down at the VFW, wanted to show up in force. Could use you."

Dell squinted at Joe. "Aight. What do I need?"

"Grab your pistol and rifle. We can worry about everything else later."

* * *

A brick building nestled between two World War II howitzers, the VFW stood uphill on a long dirt road off of Bayside Beach Road. When Joe and his team pulled up to the hall, dozens of cars and trailers and a few mobile homes idled in the large parking lot that sat off to the right of it.

Last month the gathering had looked little more than a guys' outing with some beers, but this, this was a serious meeting about moving forward, about moving up and branching out. And today, everyone they could muster was on site.

Joe had tried to rally survivors before, but most often they had gone dark—either sheltering in place or heading for the mountains. Whether they had made it or not, Joe had to believe that they were safe and in a better place.

As they walked into the VFW Joe scanned the dimly lit banquet hall. At the rear of the room he watched as the workers scurried about carrying trays of food. The meat and vegetables looked enticing, but the stink of too many men with too few showers ruined his appetite.

The right side of the hall had been partitioned off into what appeared to be a small triage area by a handwritten cardboard sign that said "Medical." In the remainder of the hall, foldable tables were out and covered in plates, rifles, and pistols. Small teams of men, young and old, sat around conversing. A few men stared at Joe's team, yet still appeared to be deep in their own discussions.

To the left of the entrance was the door to a small bar. Joe approached slowly and pulled open the door. Before they entered, Joe quietly told his team, "This guy seems to have his shit together. Try to be civil, but don't get comfortable. Lots of guys here today I've never seen before."

"Oh boy. Wonder who that's aimed at," said Dell.

Tim leaned toward Dell. "Fuck. Off."

Dell scanned the room. Joe could tell Dell was silently counting, as he had so many times before on his crabbing boat. As Dell's head turned back into sight he grinned awkwardly. "Easy to be civil when everyone is strapped."

As they approached the bar, they were greeted by cold stares, quite different from the old men that typically smiled and joked with Joe when he used to stop in from time to time—*before*. A couple other men stood leaning over a map in a heated debate. Tim whispered to Joe, "This their command center and we're now, what? Pasadena's Seal Team 6?"

A man at the center of the group glanced up at Tim. Tall, over six foot, with a medium build and sandy blonde hair. The man was clean shaven and he had a scar that ran down the left side of his neck. He wore a loose-fitting t-shirt with the words OCTAVE FUSION curved atop a seal trident. The man approached Joe's group, smiling. "Yeah, something like that. I'm Pat, by the way." The man extended his hand and Joe stepped forward and shook it.

"Glad to put a face with the voice from the other day. I'm Joe. This is my brother, Ryan, and my cousin, Alex. This is Tim and Christian Seaford, Spencer Oxentine, and Dell Bauer."

Pat shook his head. "Joe? You look familiar. Have we met before?"

Joe nodded. "Maybe. Pasadena's not a big place. Where were you stationed?"

"Most recently, Little Creek down by Norfolk. Prior to that is a laundry list," said Pat.

Joe folded his arms over his chest. "Yeah, I bet."

Pat and Joe looked at each other a moment before Pat went on to introduce himself to the rest of Joe's team, which for Joe felt more like he was sizing up each of his guys.

The briefing they had come for was initiated when Alex had come across Pat while scanning the ham radio the night before.

"Let's walk you guys through our current plan and look for any input." Pat pointed to the map on the table, saying, "Now, here on Fort Smallwood, just past the golf course, we added a checkpoint a couple days back. Hasn't been easy, and we've lost a few people, but it has held. The golf course to the right of the checkpoint has a roving patrol as well. Adding these two groups has significantly reduced the amount we've encountered here at the hall, so I'm hoping to have your group press out past there and make a run to see what it looks like farther down."

What wasn't Pat telling Joe? Why was he acting like he doesn't already have this planned to the T? Maybe he doesn't know the area that well or he's fishing for something.

Joe looked at his team. "Shouldn't be too difficult for us. Besides, my house is off of Elizabeth Road. I'd like to see how my neighbors are doing." Joe scratched the black stubble on his neck. "What else you have in mind while we're out that way?"

Pat glanced over his shoulder at one of his subordinates then back at Joe. "I have a few things in mind."

Pat outlined a few zones west of their checkpoint's location. He tapped his trigger finger on locations where they could set a perimeter defense by Hog Neck Road down to Fort Smallwood Road. Those two spots would seal their location on the peninsula by adding the checkpoints and the areas where a roving patrol would be necessary. After that, he shifted the discussion to advancing past the road block, scavenging, and dealing with people who have been isolated since the power failed last week.

Dell put his hands in his pockets and swallowed. He was squinting at the map.

Joe said, "What?"

Dell ran a hand over his head until his palm landed on and clasped the back of his neck. "Most people in this area, they probably had at least a few days' worth of food. And those who didn't, they shared. Neighbors by me have been pooling food for the last few days using up what they had in their own freezers and consolidating what they could in the freezers of the folks who had generators. Also, there's the issue of—"

"Fuel is going to be a problem," interrupted Alex. "Once everyone with a generator siphons all the gas out of their cars, it's only gonna get worse. We should locate fuel before it becomes a—let's just say—a more serious issue."

Joe pointed at the fuel station at the corner of Elizabeth Road and Fort Smallwood. "Fuel is definitely at the top of the list. Aside from those freezers, the generators are also running the well pumps that people need to get their water."

Tim was scratching his head when he looked at Christian. "Think my big diesel welder could power the fuel pumps if we wired it up?"

Christian pushed out his bottom lip. "Yeah, definitely could. Would need to find wire to tie it into the panel. But otherwise, should be easy."

"We still have that spool from the camper project," Spencer said.

"That'd work," said Joe. "We hardwire it to the panel, it should power up the place and run the pumps. What about the owners?"

Ryan said, "We'll just bargain with them if it comes to it. Same way we did in Afghanistan. If we needed shit and the villagers had it, we'd trade. Those guys loved to barter."

Alex stepped closer to the map. "So, there are two fuel stations nearby. Let's hit the one by Joe's first since it's farthest from the highway. *If* we can get the pumps up and running, we'll need to fill every damn vehicle we can and siphon them back here and at the farm."

Pat shrugged. "Sounds good. For the first mission." Pat winked at Joe. "We are going to have to start thinking about a permanent power solution soon, though."

Tim pulled out a cigarette and bit off the tan filter. He spit the filter on the linoleum floor. "Well," he said, as he lit the cigarette, "let's get our shit, boys. Daylight's burning."

* * *

The ride to Tim's garage was uneventful, and soon they were traveling down Fort Smallwood Road with the big diesel welder, tools, rolls of wire, and parts to rig the gas pumps. Alex had stayed behind with Pat to manage comms. Joe didn't love the idea of leaving him there alone with all those heavily-armed strangers, but he knew Alex was a better communicator than marksman—and, besides, if they were going to start pushing back against the Zs, they were going to have to start trusting people again.

Joe's phone pinged and Dell furrowed his brow. "How the hell are you getting texts?"

"It's the Spot device we'd use to text with when we were fishing offshore," Joe said, glancing at his phone. "I bought a few before everything crashed and gave them to a couple guys."

"Well, who was it?" Dell asked.

"Friend of mine I worked with. He's up by Glen Arm with his pops, brother, a couple of others. Dude's sort of nuts. When Baltimore fell, his first thought was to put a 50 on the back of his dad's old Army truck and do strafing runs downtown."

"Jesus. So, what'd he say?"

"Things are going fuck all, may need to evac. People looting. Biters biting. Nothing surprising."

Dell shook his head. "Fuck."

"If he evacs to us, then fuck indeed. Must definitely be a shitstorm. They are way better outfitted than us."

A mile from the gas station, Joe had Spencer pull over. Joe, along with Ryan and Dell hopped in the back of the truck. They sat corner-to-corner, giving them 360 degrees of coverage. Spencer drove, three radios sitting beside him on the passenger seat. Tim and Christian followed in Tim's service truck. They had the rear and would provide sniper cover until the area was cleared.

The radio in the front seat crackled. "Hey," Tim's voice said from the speaker. "We get cool names for this mission?"

Spencer glanced back at Joe with a hopeful expression. Joe nodded and continued scanning the woods.

Spencer picked up the radio. "For mission purposes, you'll be call sign Archangel. I'll be Reaper 1, and Joe, Dell, and Ryan are Reaper 2."

"Guys," said Alex, cutting in. "Please maintain radio silence unless calling in something or relaying movements."

"Copy that," Joe said, rolling his eyes at Dell.

"Alex needs to be less of a whiny bitch," Dell said. "We're going to the gas station, not fighting the Taliban."

Ryan shouted, "They thought it was gonna be easy on a few ops I was on in the 'stans and people died because of it. Six, if you want numbers." Ryan rested his arm across the tailgate. "Complacency fucking kills, bro. That's all I'm saying."

As they neared the intersection of Hog Neck Road, Joe radioed, "Archangel, Reaper 1, this is Reaper 2. Additional stop added. 7-Eleven detour. Supply run."

Spencer stopped the truck parallel to the convenience store's entrance. Joe told Dell to watch the front doors while he and Ryan cleared the store. From down the road, Tim called in to tell them overwatch was set.

As Joe and Ryan neared the front doors, Joe peered into the store and saw the body of a middle-aged female on the floor near the cash register. Another body lay across the counter. His heartbeat began to drum in his neck.

Joe continued to scan the dark room and noticed the girl's leg was being gnawed on by a Z. The Z was an overweight male and, fortunately for the team, hadn't noticed their arrival, because it was facing away from them, focused on its meal. In previous encounters, Ryan and Joe learned that Zs typically ignored most things while eating, but this was temporary and could end at any time.

Joe waved Ryan to fan out to the left and pointed at the target. Ryan nodded, sidestepped a few feet over to Joe's left and took a knee, rifle on the target. Once in position, Ryan glanced at Joe and nodded, signaling he was ready. Joe took a deep breath and tightened his aim as he gave a sharp, crisp whistle.

When the Z came charging out of the store, Ryan and Joe fired. The shots tore through the Z, shredding the display behind him. It fell flat on the pavement and its left leg twitched a little, then stopped. Joe waited a few seconds before moving into the store.

As Joe and his brother neared the checkout, they got a closer look at the clerk's body. He was hunched over the counter with most of his brains splayed on it and spilling into the checkout aisle. By the looks of things, he'd been shot only a few days ago. Joe looked down at the woman. There was a pistol a few feet away, laying in the aisle.

Ryan grabbed the pistol, a SIG Sauer P320. "Looks like she got attacked after she killed the clerk. Noise probably drew them in after she shot him."

"Guy was always a bit high strung," said Joe, "but he didn't deserve this."

Ryan's shoulders raised in agreement. "Shit sucks, bro. That's life."

Joe pressed the mic on the radio. "Reaper 1, Archangel, this is Reaper 2. Store's clear. Pull up to evac salvageable goods."

The store had already been picked over, but they scavenged six cartons of Marlboros, two cases of white Monster energy drinks, a dozen two liters of Coke, a handful of crème sodas, a basket full of gummy bears, and peanut butter cups. Joe grabbed a pack of Pokémon cards for his daughter Cara on the way out.

They were nearly done loading the spoils when Joe heard movement coming from the side of the store. Joe signaled to Dell, who propped his rifle along the roof of the truck and took aim.

Joe whispered, "Human or Z?"

"Definitely Z," Dell said. "Shit, about twenty of 'em coming."

Joe took a knee in front of the store to steady his rifle. "When they turn the corner, fire at will."

Dell was the first to fire. The shot missed. He adjusted his aim and fired again. The shot hit clean, taking the top of the head off. As the pack of Zs came around the corner, Dell continued firing.

Joe and Ryan opened fire from their flank, as did Tim from down the road. They had knocked down eight of them, but the remaining Zs pressed onward to the truck.

When the first wave hit the side of the truck, the impact shocked Dell for a moment and he slid back against the wheel well. Tim, Joe, and Ryan continued firing into the crowd.

Three Zs hurled themselves into the bed of the truck. Dell fired from his hip, hitting the first of them in the shoulder. The Z slowed momentarily then grabbed for Dell's leg. Dell kicked it in the side of the head, knocking it back out onto the ground.

Joe couldn't risk a shot. He pulled the Kabar from its sheath and charged toward the truck. Tim yelled over the radio, "Joe, peel off!" As Joe back peddled, the shot hit the Z, causing it to roll off the truck.

Spencer slid the M4 barrel out the window and pumped a round in the chamber. "Dell, get down!" He fired a few rounds over Dell, nailed the two Zs and sent them off the edge of the truck bed.

Joe called over the radio, "We need to get moving. Check mags and move to primary target."

Joe and Ryan ran and dove into the back of the truck, popped up and scanned the area around them. Two more Zs were heading towards them. He yelled to Ryan, "Take the dickhead on the right."

Ryan fired four rounds into the Z before it fell.

Joe took aim, looked down the barrel, and exhaled quickly before squeezing the trigger. His first shot hit to the left of center mass. He paused for a moment and, just as he was about to squeeze the trigger again, he heard a shot ring out from Tim.

Tim's shot hit the top of the Zs head. It slumped down as though it had been tripped and ate dirt. Tim called out on the radio, "Gotta hit vitals."

Joe shuddered. These "vitals" were once the vitals of friends and neighbors.

The truck lurched forward and Joe noticed Ryan staring intently at the rear of the truck, most likely waiting to see if others were going to follow behind. Dell was still holding the now-empty pistol, aiming over the side where the Zs had just been.

Joe slid closer to Dell. "You good?"

Dell shook off whatever trance he was in and sat up. "Almost had my leg chewed off. I'm just peachy, bud. Absolutely peachy."

Ryan leaned back and shouted to Dell. "Be glad you didn't have to go hand-to-hand with them like he was about to." Ryan got wide-eyed, pretended to bite his forearm, and laughed.

Dell said, "Let's just get this shit done so we can get home."

A short ride and they arrived at the intersection for the gas station. It was a typical gas station with two rows of pumps. The main building was built into a hill on the right side where the two service bays were. Aside from the overgrown weeds and a few cars blocking a couple pumps, it appeared relatively untouched.

Tim stayed parked on the road with the generator, his rifle aimed at the entrance.

Spencer rolled up and Joe, Dell, and Ryan jumped out of the truck bed. They fanned out and moved forwards.

Joe pulled on the front door. Locked. He tapped on the door and waited.

"Anybody?" Ryan asked.

"Door looks chained," said Joe. "Dell, let's check the side door. Ryan, watch our six."

Joe and Dell ran around to the side door and pulled. Locked, too. Joe walked back around front and radioed, "Archangel, Reaper 2, doors locked. Nobody's home. Need to get access, over."

"Reaper 2. Tools incoming."

Tim and Christian pulled into the station and backed up to the front door. Tim climbed in the back of the truck and fumbled through the truck box.

"Got just the thing," Tim said, holding up a broken piece of a spark plug.

"Watch."

Tim wound up to throw the spark plug when Dell leaned over and whispered to Joe, "The hell is that gonna do?" Tim threw the spark plug in the window. The glass shattered, raining a thousand shards to the ground. Dell's jaw gaped. "No shit."

Joe and Ryan went inside to clear the store.

Joe found a note under the overturned cash register.

Nina, we locked up and went to Amir's house. Come quickly. The boat will be waiting.

Love, Babesh.

"Looks like they hit the high seas," Ryan said. "At least we ain't gotta barter."

"Place is clear," Joe shouted. "Back the generator up and let's get to work. Ryan, Dell—get on the roof and give us an overwatch while we try to get this place running."

All was going well until they were nearly finished filling up the fuel tanks in the service truck. Ryan radioed from the roof, "Reaper, Reaper, Archangel, be advised. Hostile presence inbound. Approximately twenty-five Zs coming from the west and additional six, check that, sixteen coming from the east. Requesting permission to engage from the perch."

Joe radioed, "Overwatch, Reaper 1, engage target. Engage with extreme prejudice."

Ryan raised his rifle and took position. As Ryan's cheek pressed against the rest he whispered through the mic, "Game time, motherfuckers." He drew a bead on the first Z and let the shot go downrange. Ryan called out over the radio, "Drop what you're doing and clear these—"

Shots rang out and interrupted Ryan's transmission. Hot brass fell from the roof of the truck. Joe and Tim climbed into the back of Tim's truck and engaged the targets coming from the west, while Spencer and Christian were in Joe's truck hitting the hostiles from the east.

Dell radioed, "Got more coming in from the east. About 200 yards and closing."

A crack from a rifle on the roof. Then another. Ryan called out, "Threat getting closer. Be advised, three are almost to the truck behind you."

Spencer turned and fired four rounds in rapid succession, knocking down the closest of the Zs. One of the rounds passed through the Z's midsection, slowing the one behind him as it tore into his thigh.

After a short pause, Ryan called out again, "More Zs inbound from the west."

"Begin egress prep," Joe called. He grabbed Tim's shoulder. "Come on, we gotta turn this off and get moving."

While Tim shut down and disconnected the generator, Joe shoved a metal sign and a large tool box in front of the door. Joe was finishing up and noticed Tim had the wire rolled when he turned the corner and saw the Z. It glowered as it charged forward at Tim. Tim sidestepped and drew his M1911 and fired three rounds into its chest as it turned to close in. The Z stumbled and fell into a shelf of toiletries.

Tim shuddered as he holstered the pistol. "Shit, that was close. Too fucking close."

"It's all *too* close. Everything." Joe didn't turn as he spoke. "Time to get the fuck going."

Tim yelled back, "Aye aye," and followed Joe out the front with the roll of wire.

Joe fired and dropped a pair of Zs that stood within ten feet before he jumped in the truck bed with the rest of the men.

The truck sped away and Joe radioed, "Base, Reaper 2. RTB, all six accounted for. Loaded on fuel and other goodies. Be advised, small pocket of Zs tailing us. Have the roadblock ready."

"Reaper 2, Base," Alex said. "Good work, see you in ten. I'll radio ahead for the roadblock to expect you."

That night at the farm, Joe and Alex's families looked happy to see the candy and drinks from the convenience store.

After dinner, Joe walked out back, sat on the steps, and lit a cigarette. He stared off at the stars for a minute. "Made it through another day, Brooke," he said. "Not sure if this new setup is gonna work long term, but—yeah. I don't know. I miss you, Honey. You keep watching over Cara, me. Everybody. I love you."

Joe sat there for another moment, then stood up and flicked the cigarette into the yard. As he turned, he noticed Spencer standing there. He still managed a smile, but Joe knew that not everything was right with him.

Spencer handed Joe a crème soda. "We all miss Brooke. I'm sorry she isn't here with us now."

"Sometimes I think she's the lucky one. She didn't have to live through this shit. The world falling apart. It would be nice to go back in time and have another night with her back when things were simpler."

Spencer's face went flat. "I bet. She'd be proud of how you got us organized and kept us alive this long."

"You underestimate yourself, Spence. And if Alex hadn't heard about the outbreak at work, I don't think any of us would be here. God knows what the hell we're gonna have in store for us tomorrow. Let me ask you, what's your read on Pat?"

2

TWO

The next day, Joe and his guys returned to the VFW to get Pat. They had promised to introduce Pat to Joe's neighbor, Jeff Samuels, who'd been a doctor at Johns Hopkins for more than thirty years. Dr. Samuels specialized in traumatic brain injuries and had done a long stint in the ER.

After picking up Pat, the team drove down Fort Smallwood to Joe's house on the water. As they turned onto Elizabeth Lane, Joe noticed a few houses had the front doors wide open, while others had the windows boarded up. They passed a few cars pulled off to the side of the road and rounded the bend to his street.

From the backseat, Alex looked at Joe through the rearview mirror. "It's almost like time stopped around here. Not nowhere near the Baltimore dumpster fire they showed on the news."

Joe shrugged. "Not as many people. Some might not've made it home, others headed for—fuck knows—the hills. Saw old man Klebe watching us as we passed, so there's still decent people surviving this. Least I think it was him. Once we get this area cleared out, I'm sure we can get some of them to help."

Joe pulled in front of a gray stone rancher on the water. He leaned and ducked his head, searched for anything off. As he put the truck in park he told Pat that Alex would take him in. "I'm going to see if Jeff's still home. The

15

rest of my guys will keep watch out front."

"All right," said Pat. "Lead the way, Alex."

Joe walked towards Jeff's house and, as he came up the driveway, saw Jeff in the corner of the second-floor window peeking out from behind a curtain. The two-story brick house had weathered things fairly well in part to Jeff's meticulous care of his property. But like everywhere else the grass stood knee-high with weeds poking up through the brick pavers that led to his front deck.

Jeff opened the door. "Joe, how have you been? Was worried that maybe you got lost, you know."

"No, Jeff. They can't kill me off that easy. But hey, listen. If you'd be okay with it, I'd like you to come over to my house, meet some friends of mine."

Jeff smiled. "Sure, I'll be over. Let me grab Ron."

* * *

Jeff and Ron walked into the house and Joe saw their facial expressions turn fearful as they realized how many armed men occupied the living room.

Joe led Jeff and Ron to the kitchen and pointed to the small table, asking them to sit before then walking back to the living room to talk with his team.

After a short discussion with the team, Joe sat down at the head of the kitchen table, with Alex and Pat beside him. Joe introduced Alex and Pat.

"Jeff, thanks for taking the time to meet. To be blunt, we need doctors." Pat unfolded a small map on the table. "We have teams in the field trying to bring *some* level of stability back to this area. We've been lucky so far, haven't sustained any major losses or injuries our corpsman couldn't remedy. I can't overstate, however, what a boon a trauma surgeon would be to our efforts."

Jeff exchanged a glance with Ron.

"We could post an armed security unit in the empty house at the end of the road," said Pat. "We would, of course, make sure you have provisions. If things go especially well, we might be able to get power back to your house. When we need you, we'll send a group to bring you to our makeshift triage area."

"I'd like to discuss this privately with Ron," Jeff said. "Joe, could you stay as well?"

"Of course," Pat said, standing up. "This is a lot to ask. We'll show ourselves out."

Once alone, Joe spoke first. "Appreciate you hearing them out. I don't expect this to be an easy decision. I wanted to do what I could for you guys. After we're done here, I'll go next door and see Phil, try to recruit him, too. We need electricians. Hell, we need everybody we can get."

Jeff sat silently rubbing behind his ear, deep in thought. He turned to Ron, who nodded and said, "Do what you think's best. I'm with you."

"If I do this, I want to be given the liberties to set up and train people how I see fit. That said, I haven't been in the ER for a long time." Jeff continued, "I would also request power here as soon as possible. It would be good to set up a small area in the back to be able to deal with after-hours work."

"Let me talk to Alex. I'm sure he can make it happen." Joe shook Jeff's hand. "All right. I'm going to go talk with Phil. See you guys soon. Be safe."

Joe walked up the street to Phil's. After several knocks on the door, Phil answered.

"Phil. Damn glad to see you're still upright."

Phil shook Joe's hand. "Thought you'd been eaten since we haven't seen you in a few days. Had to run some assholes out of here with Eddie's help a few days back. So, what do you need? Judging by that group you brought with you, I don't take this to be a social call?"

Joe raised his hands in defeat. "Yes and no. First, I wanted to check on you guys. Second, I had hoped you would be able to help. You know, in our efforts. Jeff's going to be working as a doctor for us. And I have a lot of electrical work for you." Joe turned and looked down the quiet road. "We want to try and power up the block since I am getting a security detail up the street to watch our houses and provide a forward post for our group."

Joe leaned his head to the left far enough for his neck to crack then looked back up. "I would love for you to help us. Figure out some power solutions. Gonna be piggy-backing the houses on a diesel generator, for now. So, no air conditioning, but it'll provide enough energy for lights and refrigerators."

Phil looked around like he was trying to find the answer somewhere in the trees. After his attention came back, Joe continued. "In trade for including you, I'm gonna need to loot your feedstore."

Phil rubbed his chin. "You guys trying to save the country?"

"One county at a time. Ours first."

"What's the plan, long term," Phil asked.

"Not really sure yet. Just started clearing and found a way to get fuel. My cousin Alex and his friend Pat have a rough draft of a plan. You want to talk to them?"

Phil thought for a moment. "We are gonna need to work out some details. That stuff is a hot commodity now."

Joe's gaze narrowed as his temper started to show. "I wouldn't ask if it wasn't necessary. Given the situation, you can work out that shit with Alex. Either take my offer or I'll drive across town and hit the southern states for feed."

Phil's face showed amusement. "I'm just messing with ya boy. I'll work something out with Alan."

"Alex."

"Yeah, sure." Phil grabbed his shotgun from by the door. "He over your place?"

Joe rolled his eyes. "Yeah, he's in the house. Come on, I'll make the introduction."

When discussions had wrapped up, Pat called for his pickup. Alex had decided to stay back with Pat while Joe's team left to scout out Hog Neck Road, which was tactically important as it led to the highway.

As they left the neighborhood, Joe hit the radio. "Okay, we don't know what we're going to find up there, so let's roll weapons hot. Tim, you two keep a good distance behind us. Spence, same formation as last time. Ryan, Dell, game faces."

They drove halfway up Hog Neck, past the Brass Rail Pub and the used car lot, when a call hit the radio. "Reaper 2, Archangel. Do we intend to liberate goods from the bar as well? Over."

"Archangel, Reaper 1. If time allows we can extract on return from mission."

Ryan laughed. "Shit would probably cause as much harm as good."

The conversation was broken up by slapping on the truck door and Spencer's voice on the radio. "Be advised: Route 100 has a few Zs."

As they crested a small hill that overlooked Route 100, Spencer slammed the brakes of the truck, sharply turning to the left so everyone could see. The maneuver sent everyone in the bed of the truck scrambling to hang on.

Spencer radioed, "Be advised: Route 100 is *flowing* with Zs." He let go of the mic button. "Joe? What do ya wanna do?"

Joe looked down the scope of his rifle at close to three hundred Zs. They were swarming the far side of a black Honda Civic that had stopped on the road right at the intersection. From the looks of it, the Honda had tried to get around an accident when something had gone wrong. Inside the Civic was a young couple. The guy was trying to open the rear seats to get to the trunk, while his wife or girlfriend appeared frozen in the passenger seat.

Joe stared at the girl. Her dark, curly hair reminded him of Brooke. He remembered how she froze the same way when a black bear had jumped into the canal, too close for comfort, at the Great Dismal swamp years ago. Joe remembered swinging the paddle in an effort to scare off the bear as she sat there pale and lifeless. The bear, luckily, had lost interest after swatting the front of Joe's kayak and swam off giving them a chance to escape. But this was not the case for the woman Joe saw in the car.

Tim radioed in from behind, "We need to get out of here before they notice us. We don't have enough guns or ammo for this."

Joe's trance was broken by the Honda girl's scream. A Z's hand had punched through the passenger window and flailed about trying to grab her. As she scurried to the backseat, Joe shouted through the mic, "Fuck that! Light 'em up! Watch for the survivors."

Joe, Ryan, and Dell fired away, taking out the Zs at the hood of the car. Like Tim had warned Joe, the bulk of the Zs charged toward them. After changing out his mag, Joe radioed Spencer, "Get us moving, so we can keep some distance on them."

When the truck pulled away Joe looked for Tim's service truck and it was gone. Joe visually searched the area before calling Tim and asking where he went.

"I have an idea," said Tim, "no time to explain. Head back down Hog Neck and I'll be ready."

"On our way," said Spencer. "ETA three minutes."

Joe had lost sight of the Honda as he dropped the magazine in the truck bed and reloaded. Spencer drove slow enough to keep the Zs attention, but fast enough so they couldn't get too close. Joe slid the mag into the rifle and racked a round and began firing again on the crowd of Zs.

After they passed the gas station at the intersection of Hog Neck, Tim radioed, "Get some distance as ya pass the car dealer. And pray this works." Tim said, "Copy?"

"Roger that." Spencer pressed the gas pedal harder when they neared 100 yards away, black exhaust from the old diesel camouflaging the eighty or so remaining Zs. As they sped passed the car dealer, Tim turned out into the crowd of Zs and collided head on with them. Black smoke billowed out of the rubber tire loader as it rolled over the center of the pack.

Spencer stopped the truck, then backed up a little to give the team a better vantage. Tim turned wildly, causing the articulating center of the machine to toss off most of the Zs that had climbed on, but a few still managed to grab onto the cab and began pounding on the glass enclosure. Tim called out as he turned the machine sideways in the road, saying, "Fucking fleas, man, can't shake 'em. Take a shot when you can. I'm gonna duck under the seat for a sec., so make it count, bitches."

Joe and his guys aimed and fired while Tim jerked the wheel back and forth from under the driver's seat. A few dozen rounds had removed all but two when Tim called out, "Check fire! I'm gonna get moving again."

Dell radioed Tim, "One of the shots took the back window. One's trying to get in. Lookout!"

Tim lifted his pistol and emptied his magazine into the two Zs that clung to the top of the cab. Tim got the first off quickly but the second crawled forward as Tim stood up. He dropped his empty pistol, removed the knife from his belt, and rammed it into the top of its skull. He twisted the knife and it stopped moving. Tim pulled the knife out, tossed the blood-soaked blade on his floor, and hopped into the seat, and threw the loader in gear. He called out on the radio, "Going back to see if we can save those kids. Cover me from a distance, over."

Joe radioed, "Roger, roll it out. Have them chase ya there. I have an idea." Joe slid open the back slider and yelled to Spencer as he grabbed the Benelli M4 and a box of buckshot, saying, "Once he gets some distance on them pull up alongside them." Spencer nodded as he accelerated toward the loader.

Joe yelled to Ryan and Dell, "We need to knock down as many as possible before we get back to the car. Make 'em count and reload now." The three piled up along the passenger bedrail and waited for Spencer to have the group of Zs just alongside before he yelled, "NOW!"

Shots rang out, knocking down a few, then a few more. They had drawn the ire of the Zs and they turned to the truck. The first dozen had tripped over those that had been hit, but a few managed to ram into the side of the truck as they pulled away.

Dell stayed in the corner by the tailgate as Joe and Ryan slid to the back of the truck and began firing at the stragglers as they pulled back up to the car. Tim had drawn the remaining Zs away and had neutralized what was left with his rifle and the loader.

When they pulled up, Joe yelled, "Cover me, gonna check for survivors."

Tim met him at the Honda and grabbed the keys off the car's floor and scrambled to the back to open the trunk. Before Tim opened the trunk he shouted, "We don't bite, so don't attack us." Tim lifted the trunk open and saw the boy. He looked terrified as Tim held out his hand. "Come on, son. We need to get out of here before more come."

Joe said, "Where's Brooke?"

The boy looked at Joe as tears welled up in his eyes. "What?"

"The girl, goddamnit, what do you think?"

"They—they pulled her out."

"Why didn't you put her in the trunk? She coulda fit back there. Where is she?"

"Heather, her name was Heather. She was my wife."

Joe shook off his anger for a second and tried to be calm. "We don't have a lot of time, but if we can find her, we'll bring her back with you and get her a proper burial."

The young man got out of the car and followed Joe and Tim around the side where the window was broken out. They found her a few feet away. Her curly hair was covered in blood, while most of her face had bite marks and lacerations. Her clothes were soaked in blood and sweat, torn to shreds with just pieces left clinging to her lifeless body. Tim knelt down and verified her passing while Joe turned back from the girl and held the boy up. The boy tried to collect himself while Ryan helped Tim carry her to the bucket of the loader.

Joe radioed, "Alex, Pat, be advised coming back with one survivor and his late wife. Team's okay. Meet at VFW in twenty to hand off survivor and DOA. Have some of the guys dig a grave. Over and out."

3

THREE

"Like that dude in Colorado," Tim shouted as his arms shook around with excitement in the bar of the VFW. "What do you guys think?"

Tim had spent the last hour pleading for them to pull a Marvin Heemeyer. Marvin was a resident of Granby, Colorado. In 2004, following a zoning dispute with a concrete batch plant that would've blocked access to his shop, as well as several unflattering editorials written about Heemeyer and his being caught dumping waste into an irrigation ditch—Heemeyer covered his bulldozer with plate steel and drove through a bank, the Mayor's office, a few places on Main Street, then ended his revenge by eating a bullet.

"It's a solid idea," said Pat, "and will work well with my timeline. We need to make up as much ground as possible to get ahead of this."

"Ahead of what? And what timeline?" said Joe.

"Get ahead of the zombies' movements. As for timeline, I figure we'd plan our expansion outward to collect items necessary for my group's survival long term."

Joe shook his head. "*My* group. So what are we? Errand boys? What about the people who are running low on food and water? I don't want this need-to-know bullshit. If we're working together, we're working *together.*"

Pat glanced at Alex before turning back at Joe. "When time allows, I'll provide details. For now, daylight's burning, so back to Tim's plan, shall we?"

Joe's chair screeched against the floor as he swung it around, sat on it reverse, arms folded over the chair's back and his legs splayed. While he stared through Pat, Joe said, "All right, Tim, carry on. Let's hear it, brother."

Tim looked to Joe. His eyes were searching for a cue that things had shifted before Joe's eyebrow raised and he replied, "Go ahead, brother, let's hear the rest."

Tim swung his arm out and like he was pointing toward the door. "Right on Hog Neck Road, that construction company from yesterday. I used to work on his equipment. He has a 973 CAT loader and that rubber tire loader we could rig up. We can take the plates they use on job sites, weld up some shit and make it rain zombie carcasses all the way to I-95. We have enough fuel and they have a solid tractor over there, too—help move the track loader long distance."

Joe asked, "How do we load it in a hot extraction?"

"Run the bitch right over the side rails and zero turn it once it levels off on the trailer. We can modify the trailer to be super easy now that there are no transportation cops to fuck with us."

"Okay," said Joe, "so, balls out, how fast does that loader go?"

"It can clock twenty-five miles an hour. The 973 is going to be a mule, though. Seven miles an hour, give or take. Still fast enough to chase down some Zs. You can go out ahead on the rubber tire and come back to me and we can mangle them. No amount of bodies is going to get them stuck."

Joe said, "We'll have to mod the air intakes to prevent clogging and stalling them like that MRAP I saw that got overrun. Poor bastards tried the same thing but got swarmed, caused them to stall from a clogged air intake."

"Easy fix," said Tim. "We got this."

Alex sat with a heavy stare at the floor, his eyes moving back and forth rapidly like he was trying to process a picture that was out of focus. "So, Tim. You want to modify heavy equipment and just like, what, run over every Z that gets in your way?"

"You bet your goddamn ass." Tim held up his trigger finger. "One, it'll save us ammo." Tim added his pinkie. "Two, we have the fuel do it. More than plenty. What better way to clear a heavy presence of those biting fucks?"

Pat banged his fist onto the table. "I like it. Make it happen."

Alex said, "Take your team up, clear the lot. Then call us and we'll make the roadblock. Have to work double time, obviously, because the lights and noise may lure them down to us."

"I'll call when we're set up," said Joe. "And Alex, we *will* finish this little chat tonight. Details and all."

* * *

After a full day they had the two loaders welded and ready to go. As they wrapped up, Joe called his team together in the back of the old construction lot off of Hog Neck Road. The lot was little more than an acre of property fenced in with a half dozen pieces of equipment. To the rear of the lot was a sea container that had been turned into a trailer. As the last of his guys walk into the trailer Joe said, "Look, moving forward, keep your eyes peeled for threats. Both Z and living."

Spencer's face crinkled up. "Anyone in mind?"

Tim's laugh broke the silence. "Yeah, he doesn't trust the VFW. Well, maybe just one or two in particular."

Joe waved Tim down. "I'm not saying that. Just something feels off. I don't wanna get served up if we are being used."

"Dell back me on this," said Tim. "Joe hasn't trusted anyone since—well, you know."

Dell's shoulders rolled back and forth like he was trying to squeeze through an invisible hole. "Don't get me wrong, I don't think they are telling us everything, but I don't think they're bad guys. Tim is right, you haven't been trusting of anyone since the accident."

Joe's head jerked left and right for a second as his jaw clenched. "It wasn't an accident, Dell. She got killed."

Spencer said, "Maybe he sees something we don't. Doesn't really matter because, if it wasn't for Joe, none of us would be here. Maybe he's right to keep his guard up, maybe not. But it can't hurt to keep an eye out for something, ya know, that ain't kosher."

Tim kicked some dirt in front of his boot. "Yeah, I'll keep an eye out."

Ryan slapped Joe on the back, saying, "Only thing more dangerous than the Zs is humans. Desperation will make people do shady shit."

Joe looked around at his guys. "You're right, Dell. I'll try and keep a bit of optimism so long as y'all keep an eye out. Now let's call in that roadblock."

* * *

At his parent's farm, Joe leaned on the rail of the back porch, smoking a cigarette. He flicked the cigarette and was reaching into his pocket to grab another when he heard the door. "Ma," said Joe, "just gimme a minute. I'll even lead the prayer, but really, my head is swarming. I'm almost done."

Joe realized when he heard the tongue click that it was Alex. "Hope God is listening," said Alex. "Something on your mind?"

Joe stared at Alex. "Matter of fact, yeah, cousin. Let's start with how in the hell did you trust me enough to warn me about this plague and bring your family down here, to my childhood home, but don't trust me enough to tell me what this asshole Pat is planning?"

Alex took a step back. "First of all, I can't believe you'd say that shit to me. Second, you really think I'd risk all our lives on a god damn hunch. I knew who he was before we got there, not by name, but by who he was. I was told the guy running the VFW was sent by the same people who briefed me. He has some higher-level contacts than me, and no, he hasn't told me what his timeline is. He's kept all of it pretty hush. From the last few days, all I know is that he knew who we were and had plans for us. You need to get this paranoid bullshit in check, Joe."

Joe tilted his head to crack his neck. "Can't help but wonder what the hell he's up to. What kind of shit is he trying to get for *his guys*. I just wanna know where this is going, and I'm sorry if you feel slighted. I just, I didn't ask for this."

"I know. It hasn't been easy." Alex shrugged. "But I want you at the front of this. You still give a damn, and maybe that's enough to keep us heading in the right direction. Somebody else and this could get ugly. That's why I need you out there and me inside keeping the momentum pure. Not let it turn into something Grandpa would be ashamed of, but rather, something that would make him proud."

Joe felt his eyes begin to tear up and shook it off as he dug into his pocket and grabbed another cigarette. "Let's try this. How about as for what ya do know. Can you give me that?"

Alex's face softened. "I'm playing catch up, too, but from what I've seen it's a lot of stuff. Communication vehicles. Weapons caches from over by Arthur Slade school. And he has a bunch of shit stashed around the Coast Guard base."

Joe took a drag, the cherry on the end illuminating momentarily. "So this heavy loader thing fits right into his game."

Alex leaned on the railing beside Joe. "I need to get closer and find out more. I should've let you know sooner, but I'm still feeling him out and, for the moment, this, let's say, *venture* has benefited both groups. Soon as I figure what's what, you'll be the first to know."

"You've always been there for me, cousin. I shouldn't have questioned that." Joe scowled, "Just that, something about Pat. I don't know. He gives me a strange vibe."

"Well, I'm sure he does, because to you he is a credible threat. But don't let it own you. We are better as a team than in opposition."

Joe bit down on his cheek a little before answering. "Fair enough. Keep me in the loop. I'm beat. My bed is calling. Talk tomorrow before ya set out?"

Joe went and checked on Cara, who was in her room reading. The Harry Potter book was worn from being read so many times before. He waved for her to meet in the hallway. When Cara walked out, Joe held a finger to his mouth. "Cara," Joe whispered. "I have an idea, wanna hear it?"

Cara smiled and nodded.

Joe wrapped his arms around and squeezed. When he pulled her close, he said, "I'm gonna send you to help Uncle Alex tomorrow. But if he asks, tell him you wanted to go. I think he is overwhelmed and could use the help."

Cara kissed him on the cheek. "I can do that. Plus, it's kind of perfect. I could use a change of scenery. Everyone here is getting a little stir crazy."

Joe let go of the hug. "Okay, go get some sleep. Love you, buddy."

4

FOUR

June 4

As Joe pulled his truck into the VFW parking lot, he smiled at Cara sitting in the passenger seat. She wore her usual boots, jeans, and t-shirt. The pistol and buck knife on each side of her belt complemented her typical post-apocalyptic attire. Joe said, "Uncle Alex and *Pat* can use all the help they can get. Make me proud."

Tim sat on the tailgate of his lifted white F250 pickup, waiting. Joe parked the truck and he and Cara walked over toward him. Tim said, "Working banker's hours these days? Whatever happened to 'either you're fifteen minutes early or you're already late,' huh, Joe?"

"Dude, I'm ten minutes early and, after yesterday, I figure I earned the extra few minutes of sleep."

"Hey, Cara, how you been, Sweetie?"

"Hi, Mr. T!" said Cara. "Dad finally caved and said I can come up here today to help Uncle Alex."

Tim turned his gaze to Joe and shook his head in disapproval. "I'm sure he did, Sweetie. I'm sure they can use the help."

Joe took a deep breath. "Let's go in and talk with Mister Pat. He's an ex seal who's one of the leaders here. Uncle Alex is also working with him to figure out how we can stabilize our town. You can probably be a big help keeping them organized."

Cara grimaced. "Beats going to school. You think we will, like, ever get things back to normal? Like get the town back and you guys would be heroes and have a big parade?"

Joe stared up at the clouds before he waved Cara off dismissively. "Let's just try and survive and then we can worry about the grand vision of heroes saving the world. Remember what I said about heroes?"

Cara shrugged and mumbled, "'Heroes are in battlefields and cemeteries, and every moment that makes a hero was a tragedy until someone survived to tell the tale.' Blah, blah, blah."

Joe smiled and put his arm around her. His rifle smacked against his leg as he leaned over and kissed her on the cheek. "Remember: Be quiet, listen, and only speak when spoken to once we get inside. Everyone is pretty laid back, but they are running this like the military, minus the saluting and the usual courtesies. You get me?"

"Yes, sir!" Cara smiled and saluted Joe.

Joe's lip twitched and he tried not to smile as Cara lowered her salute. "Pat was an officer, salute him, too. Who knows, it might get him to smile."

As they walked through the VFW, Tim leaned over and spoke to Cara. "Sweetheart. So what is this, a bring-your-kid-to-work day? Because I didn't get the memo."

Cara shrugged. "Told you I convinced him to let me come. The farm is like so boring."

Tim laughed. "All right. Well, your dad told me since we're short-handed, the use of child soldiers was now authorized."

Cara gave a foul stare at Tim. "Somebody didn't love you enough as a kid."

Joe said, "It'll be good for her to help her Uncle Alex. We'll save gunning down some Zs for another time."

As they walked into the command center, Pat and Alex looked up from the maps and papers that lay scattered in disheveled piles all over the bar. Though they had a system, the only pile that seemed to have any organization was a stack of papers with names on them.

Once everyone settled in, Joe noticed that Pat had been staring suspiciously at Cara. He walked around the bar. "And who might you be, young lady."

Cara rolled her shoulders back and saluted as best she could. "Cara Wylie, reporting for duty, sir!"

Pat smiled and returned the salute. "At ease. So, you're Joe's daughter. He plans on taking you down range?"

"I wanted to come up here and help Uncle Alex out. Get you guys better organized, sir. Dad said the place was a mess and could use the help."

Joe's eyes locked onto Cara's. "Cara—"

"Very well," said Pat. "You can work here with us. Alex has told me you're smart and, if half of what I hear is true, we could use someone like you to help us get things square. You will be your uncle's right hand and help us get this place organized so we can focus on the bigger picture. Not to mention that all these old men might be happy to see a face that reminds them of their granddaughters."

Joe stared at Alex. "Now might be a good time to hear more about this timeline. And what exactly are your group's goals."

Pat looked at a map on the wall. A bunch of locations surrounding Baltimore were circled in pencil. "Simply put, we're currently trying to expand our area and collect stuff that is going be important for our continued survival. The timeline is an estimation on how quickly we get out and get it before others swoop in."

Joe's tone shifted. "Why do I feel like there's something you aren't telling us?"

Before Pat could answer, Joe's phone pinged. Everyone in the room stopped and stared at Joe as he dug the phone out of his pocket. Joe's jaw dropped as he read the message. He looked up at Alex and slid the phone across the table. "You're gonna want to read this."

Coming your way, ETA 1 hour. Rolling slow, shifter problem with M1070 tractor, can't get it to shift out of low range. Packed on heavy and trailing with about 500 Zs, request bulldozer extract like described in previous transmission. If unavailable, will be forced to waste the fucking ammo. Set up for 100 and Magothy Bridge Road. Rolling 2 vehicle convoy carrying 4 people. 3 deep in ma deuce. Personnel include brother Matt, his wife Amy and my friend James will be driving. Jen and Dudley couldn't make the trip. Can make last stand farther down if necessary. Again, we are rolling pied piper with heavy presence trailing. See you soon. Sean out.

"Doesn't read like his normal transmissions," said Alex.

"He mentioned his father and girlfriend are not coming," said Joe. "Something happened. We gotta roll. Pat, you and I are going to have a conversation if we survive this, right?"

"Yes," said Pat. "Apparently, we have both been holding a few cards close to the chest."

Joe tapped Cara on the shoulder with his elbow. "Take care of your uncle and help them get everything straight. Be back soon, buddy."

"Love you, Daddy. Be careful."

Joe winked at Cara, turned, and headed out the door, calling for his team to follow.

* * *

They arrived at the roadblock and felt relieved to see the trucks' stacks making a slow, visible wrinkle in the clear sky. Running and ready. Tim was in the track loader and Christian in the tractor. The rubber tire loader hummed on the far side of the road.

Joe said to Spencer, Dell, and Ryan, "Game face, boys. Sean's a good friend. He's rolling in hot with five hundred Zs tailing him. His tractor is having problems and we need to intercept and eliminate the threat. I don't know Sean's condition at the moment, but his girl and father are not in their convoy, which means something very bad happened. They'll be coming down 100 in the next twenty minutes."

Dell stared down route 100. "Dude, did you say *five hundred*? As in a five with two zeroes? You're talking about a goddamn battalion."

Joe walked over to the median, took a knee, and pictured the upcoming battle. As he visualized the attack, he pulled a long blade of grass and rolled it into a ball in his fingers before he squeezed the mic to his radio. "Plan goes like this: Spencer, you drive, Ryan and Dell, back of the truck facing the highway. I want you guys to park up on the on-ramp, facing away from the highway, back towards our house. When they arrive, let them pass and then light up any stragglers we don't get."

Tim chimed in, "Reaper 2, Reaper 1, Lima Charlie."

"Archangel copies," responded Ryan. "Over."

"Thanks, baby brother, watch our back. Reaper 2 out."

Ryan's voice came over the mic. "Stay safe, asshole. No cowboy shit today."

Joe checked his weapons and took a sip of water from one of the bottles in his pack. He put the bottle back in the pack and pulled out an old bracelet from his pocket. He ran his thumb over the four-leaf clover charm, kissed it, then stared up at the roof of the cab before stuffing it back in his pants pocket.

* * *

Joe stared down route 100, his mind abuzz. Sean hadn't yet appeared over the horizon, but would soon. Tim and Joe had agreed to move once Sean crossed under the overpass, a mile down the road.

Joe glanced about the few broken down cars and rotting bodies that they had pushed off into the edge of the road when he saw the black smoke from the old Army vehicles. As Sean cleared the overpass, Joe heard him cue the mic. "Punch it, Matt, and position beside them. Take a shooter's spot from the truck's rear. Make sure Amy keeps the truck running and ready to haul ass if things go south."

Matt's voice cracked as he shouted back through the mic to Sean. "For Dudley and Jenna!"

"For Dudley and Jenna," Sean said. "Ten-four. Damn the torpedoes, full speed ahead."

"Love you, bro. We got this."

"Go, goddamnit," Sean yelled into the mic. "Make it count."

The deuce and a half sped past Joe and veered to the left through the median. Sean's brother and friend, James, scurried toward the back of the truck and dove into some cases of ammo. Meanwhile, Tim's track loader sat menacingly in the center of the median and Joe waited in the rubber tire loader on the shoulder. They planned on clipping the whole pile as Sean passed. Joe prayed that they wouldn't botch it.

As Sean closed the distance, Joe and Tim floored it making the stacks on the heavy equipment throw a black cloud. Sean began to separate slightly from the mass of zombies that chased him. Joe drew a deep breath and told himself that it was now or never.

The green tractor trailer had more than 500 zombies running behind it as it passed Joe and Tim. Joe put the loader in gear and could feel his heartbeat thumping in his chest. Joe was worried. What if the rig breaks down and he's forced to watch his friends be eaten by this mindless horde? What if they run and break the checkpoints, getting everyone infected? When was the last time the oil and filters were changed on his truck? Was there a better way to do this?

He was shaken back to reality when he heard Cara in his head whisper, "You got this, Dad. Even heroes get scared." Joe swallowed hard. He strangled his steering wheel. His eyes narrowed. "Fuck yes, we got this."

The tractor sped by and Joe yelled into the mic, "Now!" The rubber tire loader jerked forward and Joe swore he saw Tim pull a small wheelie with the 973 track loader as he pulled off the grass into the oncoming mass of Zs.

The rubber tire loader and the track loader hit the asphalt and turned in almost side by side and, for a moment, as the tracks chewed the asphalt, appeared slower because of the adrenaline rushing through Joe's body into his brain. The small view holes through the welded steel made it seem as though they were looking through a viewfinder or VR headset at some impossible zombie game.

From the sound of it, Tim floored the track loader. Joe saw him pull ahead slightly. Joe pressed down on the pedal and took a deep breath moments before the first impact. He had his hand on the bucket controls and pulled back, raising the bucket to about chest level.

The first wave slammed into the bucket, exploding across the blade. The tidal wave of Zs forcing their way forward filled the bucket with halved bodies. Shrieks came from in front of the loader. Joe kept on the throttle to try to muffle the screams. The loader moaned and Joe floored it again, raising the bucket and slamming it into the road, smashing the bodies that were now trapped below it. As he raised the bucket and slammed it down again, the Zs began climbing over and launching themselves toward the cab.

To Joe's amazement, almost instantly Zs were wrapped around the cab. Out the back view hole, he saw that a couple dozen had run past them, toward the trucks. Gunfire erupted from the trucks to the rear. Joe turned back to the front of the loader and pulled his Glock from the holster. A zombie climbed into view and clamored for the viewport. Joe shoved the pistol through and fired three shots, knocking it off. The gunshots inside the metal cab left his ears ringing. He swallowed while grabbing and moving his jaw as he sat back and floored the loader once again.

Tim yelled into the mic, "Cowboy the fuck up and shoot them! If they block our view, you'll be forced to close the slide and drive blind 'til we can clear ya off!"

Another Z had managed to get up onto the side of the rig and was clawing at the viewport. Joe took aim. He ran over a pile of bodies that caused him to jerk back as he fired. The shot ricocheted off, nailed him in the chest and tore through the fabric of his body armor before stopping at the plate it held. Joe absorbed the shock and exhaled hard from the pain. He fired twice more, putting a shot through the eye of the Z. Joe exhaled again and grunted as he regained his bearings, saying to himself, "Out the window, Joe, out the window."

Joe stopped the loader and put it in reverse. He grabbed the radio. "Tim, I'm gonna back up and shake off some of these dickheads. You turn into the middle and take the mass. Spencer, how are things back there?"

Tim cued in. "Good call, start shaking them now or Dell and Ryan are going to have to shoot them off. Over."

Spencer's voice came over next. "Got a *lot* of action heading for us. Request you hurry up before we're overrun."

"Just keep shooting," Joe said. "We'll do our best. They get too close, take off. Shoot and move."

"Aye aye, Captain."

As soon as Joe stopped moving he was greeted by an ugly female Z. Joe could only tell she was female by the breast that had fallen out of her blouse.

She was howling at the loader from the driver's side port. She, in turn, was greeted with two rounds of .45 ACP and fell out of sight.

Joe leaned back, kicked the loader into motion and began a turnaround, blowing the horn. The horn elicited the reaction Joe had hoped for. The group of Zs that had been running for the truck splintered off and raced toward him instead.

Joe glanced back to witness Tim having the 973 screaming as it spun in a circle with the tracks spinning one forward and one backwards as fast as they could go.

The Zs that had targeted Tim's loader were hit hard and launched back from the bucket. Others got knocked down and were puréed by the tracks. More flew off the tracks and got mangled as the hurricane of steel spun around, ravaging the mindless bodies that continued their assault on Tim's track loader.

Joe took a deep breath as at least thirty Zs impacted the bucket of his loader. The loader shuddered as Joe stepped down on the throttle and steered toward his now departing team. Over the CB, Joe shouted, "Watch your shots as I come toward you. Start swerving back and forth as you drive away and have the two in the back shoot away from the loader. Signal Matt and Sean to follow you down 100, circle back down Mountain Road, and head toward us so we can try this again."

"Aye aye," Spencer said. "Matt is going to follow us, but where'd Sean go?"

"Reaper 2, Red Beard. Or Sean if ya don't recognize the voice. Driving back up your way. Request permission to engage from a distance."

"Reaper 2, Matt Baylor. Going to side by side with Ford pickup for the victory lap. We will continue to engage alongside your two truck bed snipers."

"Red Beard, Reaper 2. Fire at will. Safe lanes and try not to draw too much attention to yourself."

"Reaper 2, Red Beard. Won't be hard with the mess of noise y'all are making. Red Beard out."

Joe and Tim continued running over all the Zs who stayed behind to play chicken with the heavy equipment. Sean, laid across the roof of the tractor, began taking shots at the stragglers with his .308.

After the short lap down route 100, the remaining Zs were being wrapped up.

Joe called out on the CB, "Everyone fall back and rendezvous at the checkpoint. Reaper 2 out."

"Reaper 2, Base. Request to switch to alt channel, over."

"Alex, Reaper 2. Proceed to alt channel."

Joe turned the dial to channel three and waited.

"Joe, hey, heads up. I'm bringing Pat to the farm. He knows everyone's tired, but says he wants to sit down and talk."

"Okay, see you there," said Joe.

5

FIVE

June 4

They pulled up to the farm and Joe motioned for Sean to park the tractor behind the garage because it shielded the tractor from view on the road. Sean drove his tractor behind the detached two-story, two-car garage, and everyone in the house had gathered on the back porch, staring blankly at the tractor and the deuce.

Greg pointed at Sean's family. "What's going on here? And where the hell you guys been all day?"

"Not now," said Joe as he rubbed his left eye with his palm and walked toward the house. "I will explain everything soon enough. For now, this is Sean, Matt, Amy, and James. They are joining us for dinner and will be staying here until we can find them a house. They have sleep quarters in the trailer, so it won't cramp anything."

"No sweat," Greg said. "How are they on food and supplies?"

"Let them stretch their legs and then once Alex gets here with Pat and Cara, we'll hammer out the details over dinner. Mom, you mind setting places for five extra tonight?"

"Sure, Honey," she said. "God is good. We have enough to share with our new guests."

A short time later, after Sean and his family settled in, they all sat down for dinner. Joe's mom made a big country dinner with some of the venison they had in the freezer. Sean finished eating first and sat quietly drinking a glass of bourbon from Joe's stash in a small cupboard overtop the sink. Matt and his wife ate slowly and kept to themselves.

While everyone else was still working through their meal, James broke the silence. "Thanks, Joe. If it wasn't for you guys, things might not have gone so smoothly today."

Joe swallowed a heaping tablespoon of instant mashed potatoes. "All good, James, you guys woulda done the same for us."

James tried to smile. "Either way, it's good to know some people still care. We saw some folks on our way here, but none of them looked like they would have helped. Most just glared at us out the window."

"No sweat. Now where are your people at? Girlfriend, parents?"

James squirmed a bit in his seat. "My parents were in Florida. Haven't heard from them since it went dark. Girlfriend, you're funny. I'm forever alone, man."

Ryan laughed. "You're in luck. These days there's less competition. Maybe you'll find a girl, be her knight in shining armor."

Joe shot Ryan a cold stare. "I hope your family made it to safety. As for girls, consider it a blessing because it's one less person you have to protect."

"He is right ya know. Caring about people in this fuckhead world don't make it easy." Sean set the glass down hard on the counter. "Sorry about the language."

James emptied his glass of water and said, "We still got each other. That has to count for something."

Matt sat up from his plate and let his fork clang onto the table. "You're quite the optimist, aren't ya?"

After dinner was cleaned up, everyone was standing around the island in the old country kitchen when Alex and Pat walked into the house.

Alex introduced Pat as Joe's mom brought them both a plate. "Go on and eat. You all can talk after you get some food."

Alex sat down and slowly cut into his deer steak.

Pat, after peppering the meat, ate it quickly before jumping up and washing off his own plate and thanking Joe's mom for the meal.

After Alex finished his dinner, everyone sat around the kitchen table, waiting patiently for Sean to tell them about how they ended up in Pasadena.

Pat broke the ice with Sean and said, "Take your time. We just wanna know what happened and how things are in the surrounding areas."

Eventually, Sean stood and started speaking like he was giving a formal briefing. "Thank you for having us here. Today. On this fine evening. You know by now that we ran into a lot of unfriendly faces—ugly faces, really, yellowed teeth, some missing eyes and smelling like rotten cabbage, I mean just really gross stuff—and anyway, where was I? Oh, right. Many of them followed us here. And damn, it was a drive from hell, that's for sure."

Sean walked to the sink and reached for the bottle of Jack Daniel's single barrel and poured two fingers into the glass. "We were making due where we were. Hell yes, we were. Had some solar chargers and enough diesel to run generators for showers and cooking, but Dad, my pops, smart man, humble about it though, you know, he insisted that we keep two bug-out rigs in the barn across the road." Sean reached up to wipe his eye.

Joe could tell that the replay in his head was far harder than Sean had let on in the text from earlier that day.

"Seemed like we were going to miss most of the big herds, far out as we were. That is until my girl Jenna came running into the house a few nights ago. Man, she was being chased by about a half dozen of what appeared to be gangbangers-turned-Z. I shit you not."

Sean swallowed down the remainder of the glass. "We managed to eliminate them without casualties, but Dad, he got antsy. He'd seen some plans from his company, which is why we didn't follow the primary evacuation order and had chosen instead to shelter in place."

"What company had plans for this, if you don't mind my asking?" said Alex.

Sean's face looked tired as he drew a breath. "My dad worked for a DOD contractor that made equipment for them. Some of the executives had received word from the upper echelon about things and since Dad was mid-level management he got a heads up, but no parachute like their fuckhead board members."

Still standing by the sink, Sean grabbed a paper towel and blew his nose. "Then we made another huge error by shooting every one of them we came across, thinking they were the only ones around. Man, this drew in a massive amount of them. I mean, they're attracted to loud sounds. And these facebiting fuckheads, I mean, sorry for the language. That was uncalled for. It's just these—man, these, these *things* have pretty decent senses for being, you know, dead." Sean began pacing around the edge of the kitchen table, back and forth. "So they surrounded the house and we had to choose between spending all our ammo or follow Dad's orders and make a break for it while he created a diversion. His plan was simple, and he argued that since he had a bum knee he wouldn't be combat effective." Sean's voice cracked. He paused and wiped his eye. "Fucking allergies," he said. "Sorry, language, I know. Christ. Sorry."

Sean walked over to the window facing the back yard and looking away from the group said. "Dad had managed to acquire some C4 and a couple of homemade detonators while overseas. He drew as many away as possible using one of his drones. God, he loved playing with them. Used it and drew a few thousand of them away from the house, and when he set the drone in the middle of the swarm and hit the trigger, it damn near pureed the whole group. Then he ordered the rest of us to get the fuck out and he took off toward the Bobcat with a small duffel and the AR we'd built. I tried to go after him, but they held me back."

Sean took a deep breath. "He drove into the crowd, balls of frigging steel, shooting through the plexiglass windshield, making as much noise as possible. So we grabbed our go bags and hustled toward the trucks. Dad ran the Bobcat into the propane tank on the side of the house, and he must have hit the trigger for the remaining C4 in his bag. Made a monster explosion."

Joe looked around the table. Joe's mom was wiping the tears from her eyes, while everyone else sat there appearing as dumbfounded as Joe felt.

"The shockwave knocked us to the ground. And I went to help Jenna up, but I saw that she—" Sean chewed on his bottom lip. "A piece of fucking brick had hit her." The look in Sean's eyes was the same as those in James and Matt's, more tears welling up as he choked back the pain, but he blinked

41

it away and kept going. "I—I just left her there, man. I left her. I should have brought her, but the side of her head."

Sean's voice faltered.

Pat spoke up. "You made the best decision you could with the info you had. Had you tried to carry her, you could have been run down and neither of you would have survived. I didn't know your father, but I know you did what he would've wanted."

Sean wiped his eyes. "Exactly. You *didn't* know him. So, the fuck you know about it?"

"Sean," said Joe, "nothing I can say will make this better. But I am truly sorry that you had to go through all that, everything, but your father's sacrifice put you here and that means something. Something pretty big, you ask me. Take some time to rest. Get your head—"

Sean slammed his hand on the table. "Screw that, man. I didn't roll down here with my family's armory loaded in the fifth wheel and all of our stores to just pick vegetables. No offense. What I need is to get down range."

Pat's eyes narrowed. "Son, let me put it to you like this."

"Don't 'son' me." Sean shook his head. "Nope."

"Okay," said Pat. "*Sean,* what I'm getting at is you *should* take some downtime, but it will be working with Alex and me planning out the next few ops. Once we get that done, we can set you up with Joe and get you acclimated to their style of doing things. It's not like anything in a field manual, but it works for this situation."

"Yeah, we'll see," said Sean. "If I do this, I do it for Joe."

"It's settled then, soldier. See you at the VFW at 0700?" Pat stuck out his hand.

Sean looked down at Pat's extended hand. Someone at the table coughed. Someone else sniffed and cleared their throat. The floor creaked as Pat straightened his posture, his hand still out and unanswered. Sean glanced at Joe then grabbed Pat's hand. "All right."

"Good," said Pat. "Real good." Pat folded his arms. "Something I've been wondering: The Key Bridge, is it still usable? I'd like to know what's going on north of there. What do you think, Alex?"

"Absolutely. I'd also like to know the condition of the area near the fuel terminals, around the power plant."

As Joe watched the exchange, he saw something slap against the window. The noise sent the family husky, Koda, barking. The window shattered and Joe jumped up and pulled his pistol as he raced across the kitchen. Joe fired three rounds through the broken glass into the Z.

Alex met him by the window. "How many you think are out there?"

"Don't know."

"What are you waiting for?"

Joe leaned his head toward the window to listen. "Wanted to hear if the horses were making noise. I'm going, you watch the door."

Greg yelled to Joe, "I'll get the bleach and try and disinfect this before boarding the window."

Joe told Alex, "Keep guard up here. I'll sneak out the garage door and come around behind 'em if there's more."

"Let's go, I got your six," said Pat.

Joe ran down a short flight of steps into the garage while Alex kept watch at the door. When they got to the garage door, Joe opened it enough to slide under. As Joe slid under, he heard the shots.

Pat followed Joe with his pistol out and they turned the corner to head up the deck.

They reached the deck and saw Alex firing out the door as he held it shut with his shoulder. Joe and Pat began firing into the crowd of Zs the shots had drawn. The first Z dropped quickly and sprayed blood all over the siding of the farmhouse. The remaining three turned toward Joe and Pat. Joe dropped his magazine and reloaded as Pat fired at them. Joe pulled the slide back, chambering a round, and shot the last Z on the deck. After six shots into its chest, the Z crashed onto the deck. Joe holstered his pistol and moved toward the Zs they had just shot.

Alex came out behind them. "What the hell. Haven't seen any Zs down here in a while. They from around here?"

Joe rolled over one of the Zs with his foot and reached into its back pocket. "This one is from up the street. Maybe someone got desperate and broke into his house, letting them out. Check the others."

Alex reached down and grabbed for the back pocket of one of the others. As he pulled the wallet the Z reached up and grabbed Alex's arm. Before Joe could get his pistol out, the Z bit into Alex's forearm.

From Joe's left, Pat fired a shot into its head and Alex tore his arm away from the Z's teeth. "Fuck, fuck, fuck, fuck, fuck, shit. It fucking bit me!"

Pat pushed Joe out of the way as he yanked his belt out of his pants and using it as a tourniquet on Alex's bicep. He handed the end to Alex and said, "Pull it tight and hold pressure. Joe follow me!"

Joe raced behind Pat as he opened the garage door. Inside, he grabbed an axe they had passed earlier and told Joe, "We gotta do this fast or he's fucked."

Joe followed Pat back up the deck stairs. When they got to the top, Pat said, "Alex lay down and extend the arm. We gotta do this before it spreads."

Alex's face was white and his whole body was shaking, but in a breath he laid down and extended his arm. Joe ran to Alex's side and grabbed the belt pulling it tighter, then put his other hand in Alex's right hand to hold him still.

Pat swung the axe into Alex's elbow, severing most of the flesh in one hit. He swung back and hit it again, completely removing the forearm and hand.

Alex bit down as the screams of pain errupted through his teeth. He squirmed on the deck, and released one last guttural moan before passing out from the pain.

Everyone in the house had come outside.

Pat told Spencer to get the truck. Spencer ran inside and returned with the keys as he darted down the steps.

Pat said, "What blood type is he?"

Joe froze realizing he didn't know.

"I'm O negative," said Greg. "I'll go with them."

Pat lifted Alex with the help of Matt, Sean, and James. As they loaded Alex in the truck, Pat told Joe, "Get this cleaned up and check the area for more loose Zs. I'll be back to update you as soon as we get him dropped off. I think he's gonna make it."

Pat tore off in Joe's truck, tires screeching as it slid onto Fort Smallwood

Road.

Joe felt hazy as he looked at everyone. "Pray for him, but in the meantime, Mom—you and Cara watch the kids. The rest of you, let's get this cleaned up and some plywood over the windows."

Joe lit a cigarette, telling himself that *Alex was gonna be okay. Alex had to be okay because there was too much left to do.*

Joe turned to see everyone moving quickly to remedy the situation. All but Sean. Sean was watching Joe. He stared at Joe and said, "Let's focus on getting this shit cleaned up."

After nailing plywood over the back windows, everyone had sat and waited for Pat's return.

* * *

When Pat and Spencer got back, Pat said to the group, "We think we got it in time. Greg and Alex's wife stayed there to provide blood and be there when he wakes up. Doc got him sealed up and now all we can do is wait for news. Until then, let's try and focus on what we were talking about before things went sideways."

Joe's mind was still clouded, but he looked at Matt. "So, Matt, the Key Bridge? How was it and the surrounding areas?"

Sean's brother, Matt, who to this point had been staring into the corner of the room, suddenly gave a start. "Baltimore's outskirts are overrun, but the area near the fuel piers appeared to be in decent shape. Well, from a distance. Nothing burning, anyway. As for the power plant, no idea. There was no smoke from the stacks. There were still National Guard vehicles parked by the gates. Don't think they were manned, though."

"I'm curious," said Pat. "What kind of hardware *did* you bring?"

Matt grinned. "Some basic fireworks. Fourth of July stuff. Sean, wanna go show 'em?"

Sean sat up. "Yeah, we need to get out there and get some sleep soon anyway."

Sean glanced at Pat, then Joe. "It's only two-thirds of our cache, but it should help. Also brought a ton of expired and soon-to-be expired MREs that my dad had. Plus my reloading equipment and some other things. You'll dig it, I think."

After the group fanned out and moved around behind the garage, Spencer stared at the trailer and asked, "You said this thing is like a camper?"

James said, "Sort of. It's more like a mobile armory. Sean's old man made a badass rig for times like this."

Sean patted James on the shoulder. "Fuck yeah, he did. It'd be easier to just show 'em. Let's boogie before we draw more Zs." Sean pulled out a small ladder and led them inside the forty-foot sea container through a door on the side of the trailer. He climbed up and hit a light switch that illuminated the room.

Inside, the trailer had been converted into a fifth wheel camper. The front had six bunk beds, each with storage underneath. By the looks of it they were old rack systems from the berthings off a decommissioned Navy ship. Above the beds was a ladder and hatch leading to the roof. The small lockers beside the racks were filled with neatly hung clothes. A small table stood in the center of the trailer with a storage area underneath, which was packed with water and MREs. On the opposite side, a small propane grill and a refrigerator.

Sean led them through a door in the back of the trailer.

"Motherfucker," Joe said, looking around in awe. "You have enough guns, ammo, and food to supply a marine expeditionary unit for an entire deployment."

"Better safe than sorry," Sean said. "We lost close to 120,000 rounds of each caliber in the blast, not to mention two dozen good weapons, including the Armalite 50. But I did bring Dad's Barrett M107A1." Sean pulled a ledger from a peg on the wall of the container. "Here's what's onboard. We are also heavy two ARs and four pistols."

"Do you have a generator for the trailer?" Joe asked.

"Underneath. We also have a campsite hookup for it."

"Good. We can tie you into our grid system. Can't run the air conditioning, but we could get your fridge up and running. Also, should we split up this ammo a little in case we get hit with another 'oh, shit' moment?"

Sean nodded. "We'll figure it out later this week."

Ryan, who had been standing quietly, walked over to the pistols. "Think we could borrow a few of these? My rifle is dependable, but I wouldn't mind an extra pistol for the next run."

James picked up one of the Kimber 1911 pistols. "Would this work for ya? This is my spare, but I've been wanting to carry a 9mm instead."

Ryan grinned. "Fuck yes, it will work."

James checked the magazine and before handing it to Ryan said, "Take good care of her."

Ryan grabbed the pistol and slid it into his waistband. "Let me think about it."

"Dick."

Ryan winked at James.

"This will be a huge help, Sean." Pat said, "Why don't you all settle in and I'll grab you in the morning. By the way, James and Matt, what's their role?"

Sean thumbed his chin for a moment. "After yesterday and today, Matt probably wants to stick around the farm with the wife. James will roll with me. He was a 19K tanker in the Army with me, but we're both good with a rifle and a pistol."

After everyone else called it a night, Joe went and got Spencer. "Let's take a ride to check on Alex."

When they got to the doctor's house, Joe lit a cigarette and said to Spencer, "Go ahead, I'll be in in a minute."

Joe sat there hoping it wasn't more bad news.

After he finished his cigarette and flicked the butt onto the street, he saw Greg coming toward the truck. As he got close, Joe could see Greg's arm was bandaged from giving blood.

Greg said, "Lost a lot of blood, but he should make it. They have him on an IV now. Best to let him rest."

Joe exhaled hard feeling some of the stress leave his body. "Good to hear. You coming back with us?"

"Yeah, but I'm gonna head back with clothes and stuff for Alex. I'll stay here with him 'til he's ready to come back."

"Thanks, old man. Let me go in and check on things."

"That works. I'll be in the truck."

Joe walked in, saw Jeff and asked, "How is he?"

"He should be okay. It was quick thinking to take the arm, and good you brought Greg to give him blood, but we really won't know how he is for a few days. If his fever spikes, he might be infected. Other than that, we'll have him sleep away from others for a few nights—just in case."

Joe thanked Jeff, then walked in to see Alex in the small triage room set up at the back of the house. Alex was laying awake. He turned and said, "I knew your stubborn ass would be here before long."

"Ah, good. So you're okay?"

Alex glanced at his missing arm. "I'm lighter. Like a goddamn cheetah. Best weight loss program I've ever tried."

Joe tried to laugh.

Alex shook his head. "But don't you worry, I'll be back to work soon. Someone needs to keep you children on task."

Joe felt the left side of his lip curl up to smile. "And I'm the stubborn one?"

6

SIX

June 12

Joe's crew pulled up to the VFW and Cara walked out to greet them. She was dressed differently today. She had Joe's USS NASSAU hat on with her hair tucked underneath. She had on her ballistic vest, her pistol holstered, and her rifle slung diagonally across her back. Joe couldn't help but smile at seeing her like this. And even though she was surrounded all day by grizzled veterans, Joe felt hardly bothered by it. *Hardly.* The vets all seemed drawn to her, treating her like some kind of mascot.

"You're not gonna like what Uncle Alex has in store for you today," Cara said.

"Terrific," Joe said as he hugged her.

As they walked inside, Joe eyed Alex, who appeared lost in thought. "You really weren't kidding. Glad to see ya made it in."

Alex caught Joe's gaze on his missing left forearm, causing him to jump up and knock a pile of papers on the ground. "I'm okay. Good thing Cara is here to give me a hand. So you can stop staring at mine."

"Definitely haven't lost your sense of humor."

Alex scoffed. "No, not yet. But you might after you hear where we got you headed."

Pat sat at the bar on a stool, behind a map and stack of papers.

"Where to today?" asked Joe.

Pat punctuated his words, clearly lost in thought. "We need to—see how bad the city is. The military depot on Ordnance is of—particular interest. Now that your team has had a chance to work out the kinks, I want to start pressing you guys downrange—and be the tip of the spear for our push. The depot will be the best spot to start. After, I want you to hit the armory next to Arthur Spade Catholic School on the way back. They're likely both picked clean already, but we, um, we got to cross our t's and dot our i's, yes?"

Hands stuffed in his pants pockets, Joe said, "Sounds like a great place to get us killed by whatever's left of the National Guard."

Pat straightened his posture. "I would have bypassed the armory, but your friend Sean won't share his weapons with my guys, only yours. If there was an easier way, we'd go that route."

"Fair enough. But if the armory is still manned, those fuckers will shoot us."

"Point taken. If you are able to secure a few heavy movers from Ordnance Road—Humvees, mobile command centers—it'll give us better comms range." Pat held his palms up, saying, "Or how about this: You come pick me up, and I'll deal with the National Guard."

Joe took a stool next to Pat. "Glen Burnie by truck? I don't know. Seems like a bad idea. You saw how many Zs Sean dragged behind him driving the outskirts."

Pat said, "What are you thinking?"

Joe cracked his neck then looked at his team. "I don't know. I just hate getting that far out without any support."

Tim strolled over, staring at the map surrounding the depot on Ordnance. "Other problem we got over here is the prison. Could be shitbird survivors who'd want our stuff."

"And if it comes to that, bet your ass they'll get dealt with," said Ryan.

Spencer and Dell sat quietly while Joe turned to Pat, saying, "See, it's not a problem of going. It's an issue of potential fucked up surprises that we need to be prepared for."

"How about you take four guys from our ranks," Pat said, signaling to one of his men at the door. "Couple of them you've met already."

Four men walked into the meeting hall and shook hands. The first guy was stout, pushing 5'7" and sporting a high fade crew cut and miscellaneous tattoos covering both arms. He wore a Motörhead t-shirt with cut off sleeves, Carhartt work pants spotted with oil stains, and a pair of work boots with neon green shoelaces.

"Yeah, yeah, yeah!" he said. "How you doing, mang? Matt Howard." He stuck out his fist to Joe and Joe reciprocated, giving him a fist bump. "Course my friends call me 'Crazy,' whatever that means, yeah. Nice to meet ya. Let's hope shit doesn't get *too* hot while we out there. But hot enough to keep us awake, yeah?"

Joe blinked twice. "Sure. So, what did you do in the service?"

"Me? Shit, mang, was a truck driver. Used to drive big rigs through the Shitistans and Iraq before I caught an OTH discharge for, let's say, petty dumb shit. Government has no problem feeding you painkillers, but Lord forbid you shoot 500 milligrams of test and suddenly you're a monster."

"Test?" said Joe.

Crazy tilted his head slightly and shrugged. "Testosterone. Shit our bodies produce naturally. It's insane, right, like they might as well be outlawing blood. All good though because after that Abu Ghraib shit, they let me slide through the cracks. Figured that since I cooperated-*ish* and they didn't need another scandal," said Crazy, his left eyebrow raised, "so they just sent me packin'."

"A scandal? What, were ya selling the shit, too?" said Joe.

Crazy Matt snickered. "Helping our guys stay ready. Besides, ain't like there is shit to do over there but jack it and get swole. Shit's like prison, except we get guns."

Joe's eyes widened. "All right. If Pat vetted you and you can drive, welcome aboard."

"Mang, shit, you worried? Don't be worried, don't be worried. It has tits or wheels, I can ride it, mang. I can ride it."

Tim and Ryan laughed.

"Good." Joe chewed the inside of his cheek. "Good."

The second guy stood over six feet tall, had a medium build. He wore cargo shorts, tennis shoes, and a faded t-shirt, looking like he'd be more comfortable with a surfboard and a bong than a Bushmaster. He swept his long, blonde hair back out of his eyes and shook hands with Joe's crew. He beamed like the world wasn't full of roving hordes of dead people ready to snack on your insides. "What's up, dudes? This oughta be a fun ride. Name's John."

Pat introduced the next guy as "Sarge" and explained that he'd worked on tanks and heavy equipment during Desert Storm. He stood at 6'2" and pushed 250 pounds, head razored down to his skin. Some neck tattoos, plenty of arm tattoos, and a couple tattoos on his knuckles. Time had caught up to his stomach, but he still carried it well.

Sarge shot Joe a cold stare. "Need to be clear that once we get this job done on our end, that's it. My guys have their own runs to take care of."

Joe said, "All right," then extended his hand and Sarge shook it.

When the fourth guy was up, Joe said, "Jimmy?"

The guy squinted at Joe, then smiled. "Damn, son, it's been a while. Where the hell you been?"

"Here and there. Back in town for a while now, actually. You?"

"Marines, then some contract work. Had a kid. Became a cop. Wife was working as a nurse and got bit. She had the wound cleaned, things seemed good. But after she came home she got the fever and wound up biting my daughter."

"Fuck, man. Brutal."

"Is what it is."

Joe glanced around. "Oh, and guys, this is Jimmy Schmitz."

Nods and hellos were given.

Joe raised an eyebrow at Alex.

"What?" Alex asked.

"I'd like Pat to come along for this run, too. Could use an extra gun and you can lead your guys setting a perimeter while we get the equipment up and running at the depot—if there is any. Wouldn't hurt to have Pat there to negotiate, too, if the Army is still present." Joe locked eyes with Pat, saying, "You can be lucky number thirteen."

Ryan said, "Fuck, we're all gonna die."

Pat's eyes tightened, almost imperceptibly. "I'm not superstitious, so if your gut is telling you to add one more, then I will oblige. Besides, I like the idea of going out. I've been trapped in here and could use a change of scenery. Alex and Cara can handle everything here until we get back. My only request is once we get there, let us hold the perimeter while you guys get the vehicles started."

Joe said, "Sounds good."

Pat hopped off his barstool. "I'm gonna gear up. Be loaded in ten and we'll head out."

* * *

As Joe waited out front for Pat, his whole team stopped to look when Pat finally emerged. He was dressed in his issue cammies. His chest rig was a plate carrier covered in mag holders and M203 rounds that were all full. He also had two knives and a half dozen hand grenades with tape wrapped around them. He carried an M4 with a short barrel, and a suppressor. On top of the rifle was a 6x48 ACOG scope with a hologram top sight. Holstered on his hips, a pair of a HK MK23s, one of them suppressed. His gear looked heavy, but he wore it well.

Pat climbed in the back of Joe's truck and sat against the cab next to him. Dell and Ryan took position in the rear. In the cab, Spencer sat behind the wheel, Jeff and Matt to his right, respectively.

Tim was driving with Christian beside him. Jimmy, Sarge, Sean, and James were in the back.

Loaded and ready, they headed to the depot on Ordnance Road. The road to the depot was a fairly straight two-lane road. The military depot was a small location which housed about thirty vehicles behind a tall fence. The main building appeared to be more of an administrative building because it showed no signs of manning and had no barriers or guards posted as they neared it. The depot sat between a medium-security prison wrapped in razor wire and a park with six baseball fields. Across from the military depot was a large shopping center with a Costco, Home Depot, and a pet store. Pat pointed at the shopping center. "Once we clear out this area we need to send the secondary teams up to salvage what we can."

Joe motioned past the Costco. "Up the road is a few more stores and a Wally World. All would be good to hit, really. Let's get these trucks running first." Joe keyed the mic. "Tim, fall in behind us. We're going to take a victory lap to check the area."

After a couple laps, the few Zs that had popped up were eliminated and it was time to open the gate and start the trucks. Joe radioed Spencer, "Take the gate after we get out."

"Old girl ain't gonna like that," said Spencer.

"Be gentle then."

Spencer stopped the truck. Pat, Joe, Ryan, and Dell jumped out and took positions away from the truck as Spencer threw it in reverse and floored it.

Joe's truck slammed into the gate. The chain holding the gate shut didn't budge and the truck's reward was shattered taillights. Spencer pulled forward and the bumper bent out slightly. Over Joe's shoulder he heard Pat shooting and then radioed, "Hostiles, ten o'clock, multiple targets."

Joe fired on the Zs. As he dropped his mag, he called out, "Tim, get over here and open the gate."

The steady stream of gunfire muffled Tim's response. "Christian is coming, hang tight."

Spencer started firing out the driver side window when Joe noticed a decent size group heading down the road. Joe called to Spencer, "Spin her around and do what you can to draw them away."

Joe, along with Pat, Dell, and Ryan, jumped in the back of the truck. As Joe's group sped away, Tim backed his service truck up to the fence to shield the others.

As Joe faced forward, he saw the pack of Zs crossing Ordnance Road toward the parking lot of the Home Depot and he yelled over the mic, "Spencer, stop!"

The truck skidded to a halt and Joe and his guys fired into the mass of Zs, dropping them fast, but the pack continued forward at an increased pace.

When the Zs got within fifty yards, Joe yelled, "Keep them in sight so they trail us. GO, GO, GO!"

Spencer drove slowly into the parking lot as the team continued to fire. He was paying more attention to the guys in the back more than where he was going.

As Joe reloaded, he realized they had already used nearly half of their ammo. He yelled to Ryan and Dell, "Make 'em count. We are burning ammo too quickly like this."

Joe sat back and called Spencer. "Take us toward the highway, slowly. I want the sound to draw 'em all away from the others."

Tim radioed, "Gates open, most of them followed you. We are gonna keep the gate blocked and get started. Call if you need help."

"Aye." Joe took a deep breath. "Spence, hit the highway and run 'em out away from the depot. Once we get a lead, double back."

Spencer's voice shot higher than usual when he replied, "Ayeeee."

As they turned onto the highway, the mob continued its chase behind them. Spencer drove slow enough to keep them away but was starting to build the distance between them as they prepared to turn around. At the end of route 10 was a big stretch of field where the highway split around a patch of trees and connected to I-695. Joe told Spencer, "Turn her around here through the median."

Spencer sped away, giving them close to a quarter of a mile when he went to spin the truck around, saying, "Hang on!" and he whipped the truck into the tall grass. The truck hit the grass and started to fishtail before straightening out and cutting a straight path toward the eastbound lanes of Route 10. It was going well until Joe felt the loud bang and slammed into the cab.

Spencer was saying, "Fuck, fuck, fuck."

They had hit a Corvette hidden in the grass. Spencer reversed the truck and it jerked forward and started digging into the soft ground.

Joe yelled to Dell, "We gotta lock the hubs!"

Joe and Dell jumped out and raced toward the front of the truck.

After locking the hub so the four-wheel drive would engage, shots went off from Ryan and Pat. Joe ran for the bed, following Dell who dove in ahead of him. Pat winced when Joe slammed into his leg. Pat yelled for Spencer to go.

Spencer plowed forward, back into the hood of the 'Vette. The tire caught the car but brushed off as it found a grip. The pack of Zs were several feet away from the truck as Joe started to fire wildly at them. A few reached the tailgate when Pat launched something from his pack. "Nade out! Down!"

Joe ducked next to Ryan and Dell as the truck started to pull away. The squealing tires drowned out the diesel engine's scream once they finally reached the asphalt, which was when Joe felt and heard the grenade blast. The explosion had wounded a lot of the Zs but more were still coming.

Pat grabbed the mic. "Tim, we are on the way back. Status of your team?"

Tim's response was labored. "We are in, getting the trucks going now. Y'all pulled most of the Zs but we still got a few stragglers. Hurry the fuck up, over."

By the time they returned to the depot, Tim had gotten the big diesel trucks running. Christian was still working on the LMTVs (Light Medium Tactical Vehicle). Spencer ran from truck to truck, cutting the locks and chains from the steering wheels.

Joe ran over to Tim. As Tim climbed out of the LMTV, he gave Joe a thumbs up. "The good thing about military vehicles is they don't require keys. Only require knowing how to start them."

"Makes sense," said Joe. "Some private woulda lost the keys. Good luck finding a set of keys in the desert." Joe cued the radio. "Pat, one's ready. Send in a driver. We got any company out there?"

"One man coming in, no signs of Z—wait, hang on." A loud *crack, crack* echoed as he came back over the radio. "Check that, one hostile no longer posing threat."

Sarge ran to the first LMTV and climbed in. "Ready to roll."

Joe said, "Head out. When you get past the Costco, lay on the horn and leave it blasting until you hit Route 10. If you have company, floor it and blow three sharp blasts and haul ass home. If you're clear, give us two long blasts."

"Three blasts for company, two for all clear. Roger that." Sarge turned the truck out and headed down the road.

Three minutes later, Joe heard two long blasts in the distance.

Tim and Spencer got the first six LMTVs ready. Four were the open bed type, one was a heavy equipment mechanic's rig, and the other had a communication center on the back. The remaining three were being rigged up to haul the two generators and the communication unit back to the VFW.

Pat ran to Joe. "You driving one of the LMTVs back?"

"Yes," Joe said. "Ryan and Dell will drive the other two, leaving two-man teams to drive the service truck and my pickup. Why, you riding shotgun?"

"Do dead people walk?"

Joe cast him a quizzical glance, but Pat was already moving toward an LMTV. Joe keyed the mic. "Team, prepare to evac. Tim and Spencer, take up rear of the convoy. We can plow the road for you."

As they drove down the road, Pat slapped the dashboard. "You guys have been doing good. I like the way you have them trail you and then just pick them all off. Less wasted ammo."

"Don't tell me this ride along is so you can lavish me with praise."

"I need to know you are holding up, that's all. Cara said that—"

"What does my daughter have to do with this?"

"She pointed out that you haven't taken a day off since this started."

"Ah. Well, we have been running nonstop, but so has everyone else. Once we get things cleared out in Pasadena, I'll consider taking a day."

"Let me rephrase: Once we deal with this armory tomorrow, you are going to take a few days off. Try and breathe and remember what you're fighting for."

Joe hadn't expected a direct order, but he thought that now was not the best time to get into it with Pat, not while riding on a dangerous road with a convoy behind them. "And what about you?" said Joe. "When was *your* last day off?"

Pat turned away, kept his eyes out the passenger window.

7

SEVEN

June 13

As the team headed down Route 100 to the National Guard armory, Tim and Christian rode in the cab of the service truck, Sean and Ryan rode in the back. Spencer drove Joe's truck with Dell sitting shotgun, and Joe and Pat in the truck bed.

"Hope you have a plan if these National Guard guys fire on us," Joe said. "Power has been out for a month and people are getting desperate."

Pat tapped a satellite phone in his chest rig. "I do. Just follow my lead if anybody's there."

Joe yelled over his shoulder through the rear window slider, "Dell, how's it look?"

Dell shouted back, "Abandoned cars. Zs straggling off in the distance. Same old shit."

As they neared the exit for the armory, Joe asked Pat, "When are we gonna start working on getting people out? You know, families that managed to survive. Seems like all you've focused on is getting more gear for the next mission. Won't be many to save if we make it all the way to Baltimore and everyone left is a Z or has starved to death. The few new faces I've seen at the hall are all new recruits and a couple of your own. Have they found any families still intact?"

"We have," said Pat, "but the few women and children we found we chose not to bring back. We gave them food and water but sent them to other safe places. The only people we need at the hall are those going downrange. It has been too few that we have been finding, but my teams from the hall think a lot of them are hiding so we have been leaving some care packages in a few of the towns with messages." Pat took a deep breath and rolled his shoulders. "To be honest, that isn't my concern anyway. I'm hoping for survivors who can be of use. If they can't brave coming out and helping, it's just more people to take care of. We don't have the resources for that as it is."

Joe frowned. "People need to see we aren't just scavengers. They wanna see that we're saving lives, other than our own. If we can't do that how do you expect them to follow your lead into somewhere as infested as Baltimore?"

Pat stared at Joe. "Let me ask: Why do you think they follow you?"

"My guys?"

"Yes. Your guys."

"We've known each other for a very long time. Spencer's been family for years. Christ, he started dating my sister eight years ago. Tim's family I've known since we were in elementary school. And Dell, we've been friends for over twenty years."

Pat's eyes dropped into a squint.

"I mean, I don't think anyone wanted the stress of trying to coordinate and corral everyone." Joe said, "I took the job because no one else did."

Pat looked away.

Joe surprised himself that he was still talking about it. "You ever have a chief tell you some dumbass stuff, and, if you suggest a good idea, they shoot it down just because it wasn't theirs?"

"Too many times," Pat said.

"Exactly. Point is, on my team, a guy has an idea, they know it will get heard. I make the calls because somebody has to, but I'm not the leader."

Pat's face twitched a bit as though he was about to respond.

Dell yelled, "We got a problem up here!"

The trucks turned on to I-97 and were forced to stop due to a mess of wrecked cars. Joe left his rifle in the bed of the truck as he jumped out and yelled for the tow strap. Joe signaled Tim to keep back in case they needed to roll quickly.

Joe hooked a flat-tired Nissan Maxima up first. "Pull it out of the way, Spence, and I'll hook up the next one." As the strap went tight, Joe stepped back and the tires of the Maxima squealed as it slowly broke loose and was drawn out of the way. Joe was focused on the next car when he heard Dell scream, "Behind you!"

When Joe turned and a Z lunged at him. Joe shoved his forearm to its neck to keep it from biting him. On the way to the ground, Joe used the momentum to throw it past as they slammed hard into the ground. The Z rolled over and sprinted toward Joe. From his knees, Joe drew the Kabar from its sheath. As the Z neared, Joe swung the blade toward the side of its head. The swing missed, knocking the blade from Joe's hand and causing him to lose his balance as he tripped over some debris.

Joe scrambled to regain control, rolled to his back, and shifted to get his feet out in front of the Z as it charged him again. Joe drew his pistol and racked a round in the chamber. As the Z closed in, he kicked its head upward, stunning it for a moment. Joe fired three rounds into its chest, but the Z stumbled forward, its wet mouth wide open, ready to bare down. The Z made it within mere inches of Joe's raised forearm when a shot from Joe's right went through the Z's head, causing it to truly die and land on Joe.

Joe pushed the Z off and hurried to his feet. Dell and Pat were standing there, smoke faintly rolling out of Dell's barrel. Joe winked at Dell before he radioed Spencer and Tim. "Tim, back it up and get eyes on our six. Spencer, damn the noise, punch it, and let's get these cleared. We can deal with any company it draws after we clear the road." Joe grabbed his knife and sheathed it, then radioed, "Sean, Ryan. Keep an eye on us. Heads on a swivel."

With everyone in position, Joe and Spencer began clearing the road. They were halfway through the pile of abandoned cars before Ryan came over the radio. "Bro, we gotta move. Large group coming from the south. They'll be here soon. How long to get shit moved so we can get going?"

Joe looked ahead. At least two more cars needed to be moved before Tim's service truck would fit. "How long 'til they're on you?"

"Shit, bro, two fucking minutes, if we're lucky. Over!"

Joe ran the strap through the hitch on the pickup and waved Spencer to go. "One more and we roll. Tim start coming forward slowly, we'll be ready when ya get close."

Joe ran, unhooked the strap and pulled it tight as they got near the last car. The bumper was crushed under the car. Joe eyeballed the strap and knew it wasn't long enough to pull around to the front of the car, so he drew his pistol and fired a round through the back window, then the passenger side rear window. Joe ran towards the corner of the car and swung the shackle through, spraying glass on the road. As he hooked the shackle, Joe swung his arm in the air with his fingers swinging like a cyclone. Spencer floored the old diesel, pulling the last car far enough out of the way to clear their path to Dorsey Road. Joe ran to disconnect the strap and the sound of gunfire erupted from behind Tim's service truck. Joe pulled the shackle and tossed it over the hood into the bed of the truck.

"Gotta move, now!" yelled Pat.

Joe radioed, "Tim we are a go, roll it."

Joe jumped in the truck and stashed the strap into the back seat pulling up the slack as he fed it into the window. Dell climbed into the front seat and yelled, "Go, go, go!"

The trucks had gone about a half mile and ambled past Sawmill Creek park. The basketball courts and skate park had grass sprouting up through the cracks and the fencing was torn in the corner by the tennis courts. Joe stared, lost in a patchwork of memories: people riding skateboards, shooting hoops, playing tennis—a reverie broken by Spencer on the radio, saying, "Roads clear for the most part, but we are gonna run into a few Zs by the school." Joe reached for his mic but Pat beat him to it. "Ten four. Stay the course." Pat sprung up, laying his rifle over the roof of the truck and firing at the Zs in front of them. A few rounds of hot brass bounced off the bed of the truck before Pat radioed, "Threat eliminated. Continue to the armory."

The three-story brick school appeared as they rounded the bend. The building stood intact, although several first-floor windows were shattered. Joe yelled to Pat, "Could be a good spot to house survivors."

Pat shrugged. "There will always be more survivors."

Joe looked away, trying to hide his frustration. "What's the goal here if not to save people and organize them? We need to start freeing people up and getting them to help us, too!"

Pat didn't respond. As the truck came to a stop he radioed in, "Everyone, weapons low. Looks of the entrance, nobody has sacked the place. Might be survivors."

Pat and Joe hopped out of the truck and walked towards the armory entrance.

Pat knocked "Shave and a Haircut" on the door, and two knocks followed from the other side.

The door opened slowly to reveal four armed soldiers.

Pat gave the men a few seconds to assess the situation before he spoke. "Gentlemen, allow me to introduce myself. I'm Lieutenant Commander Patrick Miller. I have been given authorization under Defense Secretary McLaven to absorb any members and equipment from your units for the purposes of elimination of current threats in this county. Once the county is cleared you will be tasked with joining the acting Maryland state militia in future events, including but not limited to clearing Baltimore City and moving south to clear the Capitol."

The highest-ranking member was a staff sergeant. He introduced himself as Thomas Maurice, then took a deep breath. "Sir, with all due respect, what you are saying is a little hard to swallow. Do you have a set of orders I can see or are we to take it on faith?"

Pat didn't seem bothered. He removed the satellite phone and dialed. "Admiral, it's Pat. Need a favor. Could you to explain to this staff that we are here to load up their equipment. Can you send word through Meade. Yes, on Dorsey. Aye aye, sir."

Less than a minute later, a small private ran to the doorway where the two teams stood facing each other. "Staff Sergeant, message just came in. Code word 'ravens.' What does it mean?"

Maurice saluted Pat.

Pat returned the salute. "At ease. You did well, Sergeant. But now, we need an inventory of this armory and we need to begin loading up and transporting it to our current base of operations. You and your men will be coming with us."

Joe was dumbfounded at what he had just heard. His fury showed as he stared at Pat who returned the look with a nod.

Pat faced Maurice. "We need to move double time."

Maurice saluted. "On it, sir."

Maurice led Pat and Joe to the weapons vault where they found:

- (120) M4 rifles with 200,000 rounds of ammo and six cases of mags
- (4) M249s with 20 cases of ammo
- (4) M240 rifles with 20 cases of ammo
- 6 cases of M67 frag grenades
- 2 cases of smoke grenades
- (4) M203 launchers with 2 crates of M433 dual purpose high explosive shells
- 2 crates of M406 high explosive rounds
- 1 crate of M576 buckshot
- 1 crate of M583A1 star parachutes

Joe radioed his team. "Boys back up to the loading dock. Need to load and move quickly."

Pat asked Maurice, "What do you have for vehicles?"

"Three Humvees, one MRAP, and two satellite transportable terminals."

"Load them all, we move in twenty. Get your men loaded with all the ammo and weapons, double time."

Joe's team arrived back at the VFW as the sun started to set behind the tall pines to the west. Joe felt relieved as the last of the weapons left the truck, the offload completed. He flicked the cigarette and waved to the rest of the team to head in for the meeting in the bar with Pat.

Once all the men had gathered, Pat started. "I want to commend you all. This hasn't been easy. Somehow, through ingenuity and bravery, we have managed to get our corner of Pasadena fairly secure."

As Pat continued to talk, Joe drifted off, staring at an old dart board in the corner. He had heard everything already that Pat was about to say. Joe wondered what really was coming in two days to allow his guys a few days of rest.

Tim slammed his glass into the bar to rouse Joe.

"We managed to get a new fleet of vehicles to start outfitting other teams to work similarly to the style that you guys use," Pat said. "A style, might I add, that seems to be rather conducive to the current environment. That said, I intend to outfit you guys first, so go see Jim out back after this. He has my orders on vehicles and gear for you. Also, you guys will have Sean and James permanently in your group. Which brings me to my next order of business: vacation. Nobody else has worked as much as you guys. So, after this meeting, you are ordered to take two days R&R."

Joe looked at his team, then back at Pat. "You heard him, load out and go home. Anything else?"

"I want you and Alex to stay after for a few minutes, for a bit of planning. As far as everyone else, enjoy the much-deserved break."

The team stood and, before they could hit the door, Joe shouted out, "My house. O Eight Hundred. Mandatory fun. Don't worry, it shouldn't take all night."

They all departed, leaving Alex, Pat, Cara, and Joe.

"Okay," said Joe, "first of all, when were you going to tell me you planned on marching us into Baltimore City?"

Alex rubbed on the bandage covering the wound where his left forearm used to be. "Where are you getting this from?"

Joe stared through Pat. "That's what he told the reservists today when he gave them government orders to fall in with us."

"Alex you already know some of what I'm going to say but I will start from the beginning since we are past phase one and things will move quicker if you both know the whole story." Pat said, "Joe, as you heard earlier, I intend to roll into Baltimore, but not downtown. More along the outskirts to try and get access to as much equipment and supplies as we can before phase three."

Joe said, "Phase two is what exactly? And what happens in phase three?"

"My mission objective when I got here was to gain a leadership role among the people and organize and execute the plan. That plan was to find teams to clear neighborhoods and acquire the gear and supplies necessary to take back the suburbs around here. You saw the videos of the hordes of Zs in the cities. We don't have the manpower to take them back, so, to be blunt, phase two is acquire everything within reason along the outskirts and fall back. Then once complete in July they plan a tactical strike and razing Baltimore to rubble."

Alex sat with his jaw agape. His hand squeezed his bandage and caused it to turn red. Joe knew he was privy to more than he had let on but what Pat had just told him had certainly came as a shock. Alex released his grip on the nub and pointed at Pat. "That was supposed to be a last resort! We still have time and we agreed Baltimore would have been a perfect test since they have a lower population than a lot of the big cities."

Joe slammed his hand on the bar, causing the drinks to shake. "That is bullshit! We don't even know if there are survivors. And they just plan to level all the major cities? We need to get up there and at least give any survivors a chance to self-extract. They deserve at least that much."

Pat shook his head. "I don't like it any more than you do, but those are the orders. I can't make these guys who have survived this long march into certain death. The counties haven't been hit like the cities. It is bad downtown, and that is leeching out into the counties making their situations more dire by the day."

Alex's eyes glowed from rage, but as he turned to Pat, a calm came over his face. Joe had seen that look before. It came right before he went off. "Pat, how long do we have before they call in the strike?"

Pat glanced over at the sat phone. "July fifth. So, twenty-two days."

Joe's face turned bright red. "So in three weeks they are going to level Baltimore? What else is on their plans you haven't told us?"

"We intend to enlist and promote those who have shown promise in this new world and have them continue on after Baltimore and do the same thing in surrounding cities. Save what you can, salvage what is available and eliminate any threats."

65

Joe asked Alex, "How much of this did you know?"

Alex put his hand up, as if taking an oath. "None of phase three, only that we were going to continue on along the edges of the city salvaging what we could to keep our group and others moving to kill off the Zs. With no news regarding a cure or vaccine, at this time it's their nuclear option without the fallout."

"Joe, the risk isn't worth it to go into the city." Pat's shoulders rolled forward and his face hinted a frown. "There is a very low likelihood of significant survivors. They've been without power, water, and septic for weeks. Without any infrastructure and no support. According to what they are seeing from satellites, there is a lot of Zs roaming and few survivors."

"If I still lived in the city it's not as if I'd be leaving SOS signs on my roof."

"Our job, whether we like it or not, is to survive and reboot the East Coast. If you have a better idea let me know, but until then I want you to take a few days rest and come back ready to do what humanity needs to survive."

Joe looked at Cara who was standing behind the bar, her eyes holding back tears. "Cara, we're leaving. Alex, we'll talk after dinner. Pat, see you when I see you."

As Joe drove down the road Cara asked, "Are they really gonna blow up Baltimore?"

"Well—" Joe shook his head. "Wonder what Grammy is making for dinner."

8

EIGHT

June 14

Dell had the old diesel running on the 34 Deadrise when Joe pulled up.

Joe, Sean, Greg, and Ted pulled weapons from the truck and Dell shook his head, saying, "So much for a day off. We even gonna fish today, buddy?"

"We're gonna fish," said Joe, "but there's something we need to do while we're out." Joe handed Dell two duffel bags, a gun case, and a couple M4s before climbing aboard. "Need to go into the inner harbor, take a look around. See if there are any survivors and how the Zs move around and react when we aren't in sight."

Sean, Greg, and Ted climbed on to the boat.

They headed out of the narrow channel from the creek. Joe slapped Dell on the back. "We need to drop some cameras when we get into the harbor. After that, we focus on fishing."

"Fishing. Yeah, sure."

"Need to see what Zs do or how they act when there's no human stimuli."

"No reason we can't fish on the way," Dell said. "Start putting the lines out. We'll roll six rods on our way up, set out the rest after your cameras are done."

The general good mood during the outing even started to affect Joe and Dell.

Greg motioned toward Sean, who was asleep in the forward cabin. "How's he holding up?"

Joe leaned over and checked the depth finder, then looked back toward the key bridge. "Long as we keep him busy, he should pull through."

"We really have been lucky so far. We should play the lottery," Greg said.

"Ha, no doubt. I wish Brooke was here to see all this." Joe stared at the horizon, thinking about that day on Route 100. As the bay air rushed over his face, his mind replayed Tim's first ride in the rubber tire loader. He remembered the girl, who reminded him of her.

"Fish on!" Dell yelled.

Joe took the wheel while Dell pulled the rod from the holder and set the hook. "She's a big girl," he said. "Who wants her?"

Greg ran to the back of the boat. Dell placed the rod in his hands and yelled to Ted, "Clear the other lines."

They reeled in the other five rods as Greg fought the fish. Sean emerged from the cabin with a net as they came up on Fort Carroll. Dell got a hand on the leader and signaled for Greg to step back as Sean brought the net over the side of the boat. With one big swoop, he brought the fish in. A rockfish.

With waves lapping against the boat and the bay's salty stink in the air, the group huddled around the fish for a picture. The instant Joe felt something resembling happiness, he reflexively conjured up memories of death and suffering, both past and present, and let guilt wash over him.

A safer state of mind.

As they closed in on the channel heading into the harbor, Joe stepped into the cabin and returned a few seconds later with an M4 resting over his shoulder and a duffel bag in his hand. "Eyes open, guys," he said. "All this debris out here, we don't want to lose our ride home."

Using the high-powered scope on top of a Remington 700, Sean scanned the shore line. Next to him, Ted held a camera, taking photos and video. As they rounded a bend into the harbor, Dell shook his head. "Look at this shit." Dell piloted the old Deadrise past Domino Sugar when Joe understood just how bad things had gotten in Baltimore. To the north, dozens of docks had party boats sunk in their slips, visible only by the bridge or bow poking out of the water. Piers to the east had been torched, save a few scattered pilings, thanks to a higher tide. And while a few small flotillas of luxury yachts rocked gently, anchored off the docks, a few of them had started to list and would likely sink soon if no one pumped their bilges.

Greg raised his hands to the sides of his head, clutching two fistfuls of hair. "Jesus."

They slowly rode in closer, surveying the damage. Joe noticed a shirtless man with his hairy pregnant belly, out there wearing nothing but a pair of neon orange shorts. Just sunbathing on the deck of a large cabin cruiser.

Sean tilted his head off his scope. "Who's he hiding from? I'm mean, don't get me wrong, I'm glad he's wearing drawers. But, man, if that were me? All alone? Shit, I'd be balls out, jingle jangle. Perks of living during an a-fucking-pocalypse."

Greg laughed. "You would, too, you damn sicko."

Maybe it was the normalcy of the man's act, of catching some rays.

Maybe it was the comradery between these men, in the muck of it all.

Maybe it was a revitalized sense of hope.

Whatever *it* was, it made Joe smile for so long that his face hurt.

The men past the aquarium and rode into the main part of the harbor. Along the shore and on the docks, Zs were running in from all over, drawn by the rumble of the diesel motor echoing off the water.

From behind the scope, Sean said, "Target, one o'clock, third story window."

A couple stood waving from a third story window of the T. Rowe Price building. As Joe and the men watched, more people opened their window blinds. One woman held a sign that read: "No food, please help."

"Target, seven o'clock, roof top," Sean said.

Two guys standing on a rooftop deck above Rash Field waved an American flag.

"Now what?" Dell said.

"We set the cameras," said Joe, and all eyes immediately turned to him. "Same as before. Stay on mission."

Dell said, "Joe's got a point. Not as if we've got C-rations to throw them."

"You two fucking serious?" said Sean. "Should we also toss our poles in, pound a few beers?"

Joe winced. "Look, we don't have supplies for them, nor do we have room on this boat—"

"Hell, I know," said Sean. "Let's break out some flares and have a dance party. I mean, show them what's what. The 'haves' versus the—"

Joe held his hand up, saying, "We drop the cameras, then we'll clear as many of the zombie fucks as we can. Boost morale in the meantime."

"Whatever, man," said Sean.

Joe asked Dell, "Do you have a signal lantern on board?"

Dell nodded.

"All right. Let them know that we will be back." Joe glanced at Sean. "Most of them won't understand, but maybe a few will, and the word will spread. I don't know. It's something."

Joe asked Sean, "Good?"

Sean played deaf and turned back to the scope, recommencing his scan.

After signaling the survivors, Dell navigated around the wreckage so they could attach the four GoPro cameras to the abandoned boats.

Joe pointed ahead. "Let's make one more stop before we start dropping these things." He had Dell pull up to the forty-five-foot Carver that he'd seen on their way in. He thought he'd seen someone's shadow move on board.

"Hello?" Joe called. "Anyone here? Coming aboard. We don't bite."

No reply.

Joe cautiously climbed over the bow rail and walked toward the aft of the vessel. The door to the main cabin slid open. Joe saw a tall man with dark hair and an unkempt beard running at him with a butcher knife. Joe reached for his pistol, but was too slow. He sidestepped the man, his right shoulder getting grazed by the knife in the process. Joe grabbed the man's forearm and hammer-fisted his wrist, knocking the knife loose. The man grunted and swung wildly. Joe hit him with two jabs, a right cross, and a left hook. The man stumbled back and then charged forward, diving at Joe's knees. Joe sprawled out and the guy faceplanted on deck. Joe spun around on top of him and put him in a chokehold.

"Easy, easy. Go easy," said Joe, but the man squirmed and grunted before quickly falling unconscious. Joe set the man's head down gently, then signaled to his team that he was fine. Joe walked into the cabin. Except for a bucket that appeared to have been used as a toilet, the cabin looked empty. Joe put his hands on his hips. "Shit." He looked around again, tried his luck under the console and found a first aid kit. Joe used it to wrap his shoulder.

Back on deck, the man was waking up. With his pistol pointed at him, Sean asked, "What's your name?"

The man snorted, spat a greenish glob on the toe of Sean's boot.

Sean rubbed his boot on the man's pants. "You tried to stab my friend and all he gave ya in return was a sore jaw and a free nap. Now, before my trigger finger gets excited, I'll only ask you once more. The fuck is your name?"

"Pussy Licker," the man said, rubbing his jaw. "Your mother around?"

Sean pressed the gun to the man's temple.

"Sean!" said Joe.

Joe walked over, squatted beside the man. "You got family, Mister Licker? Any friends?"

The man stared at Joe. He blinked slowly.

"All right," said Joe. "Know anything about the zombies?"

The man shook his head. "Not really. Basic stuff. Active during the day, but'll run around some at night, especially if there is light or noise. They're fast. Pretty stupid. And people? Dude, people are just part of a well-balanced meal."

"You're saying what exactly?" Joe asked. "They got a food pyramid?"

"You know it'd be a lot easier to play ten thousand questions without a piece in my face."

Joe nodded at Sean and Sean holstered the pistol.

"They run in packs, too, most of the time. But there are some that are kinda like lone wolves. Those seem to be a bit smarter. In comparison to the others, I'm saying." As he paused for a breath, the man slid across the teak deck back against the transom of the Carver, resting his head against it. "Oh, and before. What I mean is they kill off the weaker of the group when they get hungry. Dead flesh serves as an appetizer. Like, get this. A few guys, they tried to make an escape maybe a week ago, I can't keep track. Days all blend together. Anyways, one of them was carrying guns. They got spotted real quick but the dude wasted about six of them before—before he got cornered. After that, the craziest went back and ate their own."

Speaking was obviously a chore. Joe let the man swallow and take several breaths. "So, Mister Pussy Licker—"

"Robert," said the man. "It's, it's Robert Lightner."

Joe scratched his chin. "Good. Well, Robert, the way I see it, you should come with us. We got a few guys who are gonna want to talk with you. You've been out here watching all this time. You've a rough idea who's out here, number wise, still surviving."

Robert stood up, brushed himself off, and walked to the edge of the aft deck. "Dude, all due respect, I'm not going anywhere. And definitely not with you brutes."

"He wasn't asking," said Sean.

Robert met Joe's eyes, then Sean's. "Fuck y'all. You assholes come on my boat. Threatening me on my boat. Humans are worse than the dead, I swear."

"We've got food," said Joe. "We've got water. We've got—"

Before Joe could finish, Robert popped up and jumped overboard.

Splash.

After Robert swam a short distance away, Sean aimed a finger gun at him. "Bet I could hit him with my eyes closed."

"Where's he think he's going?" Joe watched as Robert made it to the closest spot in the harbor and climbed the bulkhead, clearly oblivious to the small packs of Zs on both sides of him. Once he had pulled himself to the top, Robert turned back and flipped the men two middle fingers before being tackled by a zombie. Robert screamed until others piled on, snarling and biting, muting Robert entirely.

At the edge of the boat, Joe choked the rail with both hands. "Idiot."

Once Joe attached the last camera to the boat and waved Dell around, the men had a few hours of daylight to catch some dinner and be back for the cameras before dusk.

* * *

As the sun set behind the buildings to the west, with eighteen big rockfish in the hold, they headed back to the harbor to retrieve the cameras.

Joe had stopped to talk to the man they saw sunning on the deck of the cabin cruiser to no avail. His name was Walt. Walt had gone to water as soon as things got bad, but rather than running he had just been catching fish and pillaging other boats quietly to find supplies. The only response he had when Joe asked if he needed help or wanted to join up was, "Fuck that. Why come out of retirement now?"

As they left Walt, Sean said to Joe, "He isn't wrong. I can respect his style. Nobody to count on, nobody to lose."

When they had all four cameras on board, Joe told Dell, "Back her in, Cap. Let's have whoever's watching know we're here to help."

Dell gave a thumbs up. Sean nodded.

The boat floated in position. The guys leaned over the transom with their rifles aimed at the square. Sean was laid out across the roof of the boat with his rifle in the prone position.

"Sean," called Joe, "mow a few down in the center of the square to draw them in. Everyone else, wait until they pile up so we can maximize our bullets."

There was a small group of about thirty Zs spread out in the square when Sean fired the first shot. The .308 round tore through the throat of one, hitting another a few feet behind it. The target of the initial impact crumbled to the ground while the secondary target stumbled forward, falling moments later.

Robert had been right. The Zs downtown must have been starving because, unlike the ones Joe and his team had encountered, they dog-piled the newly deceased and chewed into it. Some of the larger Zs, however, focused solely on the boat and stood at the edge of the water screaming. The commotion sent a few into the water, doggy paddling toward the boat. Joe shot them before they got too close.

"Used to love taking clients up here after a charter," Dell said quietly, to himself really.

The square steadily filled up.

"Okay," said Joe, "let me try this 203 out and then we can do a few mag dumps." Joe loaded the 203 with a high-explosive, dual-purpose round.

"Aim high," Sean said from behind his scope. "Let the fuckheads by the water absorb the shock."

Joe took a deep breath and fired the round. It sailed through the air, passed over the first two-thirds of the crowd before landing. The blast ripped through the Zs, sending blood and body parts airborne. The Zs that weren't hit with shrapnel were knocked down by the shockwave. The crowd erupted into hysteria.

Some pushed others into the harbor, trying to get away. The Zs who fell into the water drowned each other as they attempted to claw their way out. While some were drowning, others convened eating the newly deceased.

The sound drew in hundreds more, who came charging in and feasted on the dead. Dell shouted to the guys at the rail, "Wait for them to regroup." Joe grabbed a fresh mag and reloaded as the others did the same. Dell looked up at Sean, then back to Joe, "Okay—now!"

The .223 rounds tore through the Zs and kept going, obliterating multiple targets. Shots to the head or spine dropped them instantly. Shots to vital organs took longer. The gunfire and fresh dead continued to attract more and more zombies.

The guys emptied their mags, then Joe launched another .203 round.

Sean scanned the area and reported people in windows and on rooftops cheering. Once he refocused on the Zs in the square he told the guys to wait. After he watched for several seconds, he shook his head in disbelief. "Joe, you ain't gonna believe this."

* * *

Back at the VFW that night, Joe gave a quick debrief before turning it over to Sean.

Sean took a deep breath as the rest of them leaned over the old oak bar. "This is going to sound crazy, but, man, some of them seem to still have some cognitive function. As I was scanning the harbor, I saw this one who wasn't running to the buffet. He was—fuck, tough to say—seemed like he was just watching." Sean shifted his weight to his right leg. "When the guys laid down gun fire it didn't appear too concerned, but when Joe fragged the fuckers with a .203, it ran before the round even went off. Man, I'm not saying it was smart, but it wasn't mindless either."

"That's weird," said Alex, rubbing the gauze where his elbow used to be. "This whole world anymore, of course, but that shit? That's damn weird."

"In the grand scheme, it doesn't change dick," said Sean. "But yes, damn weird, for sure."

"Would you mind going through some of the tape with me, see if you spot him?" Alex said, "I mean, I know you've had a long day, but if you're up for it."

"Fuck it. We got tomorrow off, so that works. So long as the drinks are on the house."

Pat grabbed Joe's bicep and lead him off to the side. As they stood below an old prisoner of war flag, Pat's voice was just above a whisper. "This riverine unit you want, think we can get it up and rolling for a raid on Baltimore in two days? I'm not promising anything, but if you can get some survivors out of there, it may give me ammunition to hold back the air strike."

"Let's find some boats, preferably some Deadrise workboats with big back decks, and we can set it up. We can even maybe make mounts for the 240s and use them, too. There's some other things, but they'll be contingent on you getting me my fleet of Deadrises."

Pat stood statuesque, eyes moving around the room. "I'll find you the workboats, but I have to ask: what happened to taking the day off?"

"You forced my hand," Joe said. "Couldn't let you just call in an airstrike when there are still people there. In large numbers the Zs are a serious threat, no doubt. But I think we can do it without burning the place to the ground."

"Here's the thing, Joe."

"Pat, I'm not in the mood for debate. For now, let's go through this tape and you find me some boats."

Alex fought to connect the USB plugs to the laptop that sat between them on the bar. After pushing Sean away when he tried to help, he hit play on the first video. A few minutes in, Sean pointed at the screen. "That's the bastard right there!"

Everyone crowded around the monitor and watched the "Smarter Z" walking through the crowd. On three occasions it stared at the camera.

"Son of a bitch," Alex said.

"Fast-forward to the kill footage," said Pat. "We have a long night ahead of us."

* * *

After they finished watching the footage, Sean and Alex said goodbye to Pat and headed home. Pat sat quietly with Joe until everyone left. Once Pat and Joe were alone, Pat pulled out a laptop and brought it to life. Pat tapped in his passwords and started sending the files. "It's frustrating to be out of the loop," said Pat, "I know." Pat hit the return key and said, "I was waiting for the best time to bring you in. Likewise, moving forwards, I need you to trust me." Pat turned the laptop ever so slightly in Joe's direction. "I'm sending some of this to the Admiral. Feel free to read over my shoulder so you can gain some additional perspective."

Joe read as Pat typed out the message.

The team believes they are seeing some zombies with higher-level cognition. Also, a now deceased contact in the harbor spoke of lone wolf or Alpha zombies in the pack. Looking for any intel to confirm or deny.

Pat sent the files off then strolled to the cooler, grabbed a bottle of old scotch and poured a drink. As he swirled the scotch around the half empty glass, his phone rang. Pat sat his drink down and answered, placing it on speaker. "Admiral, good to hear from you. I've got Joe here with me on the line. What do you have for me?" Pat leaned his elbow on the bar and sipped his drink as Admiral McLaven replied dryly, "Hello, Joe, and yes, Pat, there have been new developments. Let me start from the beginning and then I'll answer your questions after, as well as send you our findings.

"First, as for the so-called 'smart' ones, what we have found is they aren't really as harmful as the others. Our scientists think it has something to do with body temperature during the turning process. These ones apparently didn't reach above 105 when they had their pre-turn coma period. This resulted in some small level of maintained cognitive function. That said, they are still unstable but less likely to travel in large packs. Also, they have the ability for some minor problem solving and lack the heightened levels of aggression that the majority have. According to some recent testing, they will still reach a heightened level of aggression when a meal opportunity is presented. Or when they feel cornered. But typically, they are the scavengers of the group. They come by and eat once the herd has moved on.

"As for the intelligence, tests show they have less brain function than lab rats. Although in comparison they may seem like geniuses compared to the packs. The only time these ones are going to become an issue is when you start taking doors and roll into dark places.

"As for the alphas and betas, our snipers noticed the same trend outside of the base. We had a few of them taken out quickly and silently, but the next in line steps right in and the pack continues on like nothing happened.

"The selection process for the alpha is almost fully agreed upon that it has something to do with pheromones, but even when they are separated, they continuously form up and attack anything that isn't them. They even attack each other and kill off the pack's weakest when food becomes scarce.

"We know for sure they need water. Our contacts in the desert and mountains have noticed where there is no water supply readily available there is barely any zombie presence.

"Hope that helps. And how is your group of alphas doing?"

Pat smirked. "Surprisingly well. He has proven to be a huge asset with the group he put together. They work really well and don't seem to have any serious issues. Joe will probably take the promotion, but he has some ideas of his own that need to be hashed out first.

"As for his guys, I have no doubt they would follow him to the underworld and fight Hades if Joe said it was necessary.

"The other teams are doing pretty well. Pasadena is damn near green and we have been doing our best to get food and fuel to people and keeping the patrols working round the clock.

"That's about it, Admiral. I'm going to call it and get some rest. I'll be in touch, Miller out."

Pat hung up and sat the phone next to his computer.

"Seems like your bosses are pretty happy," said Joe. "That means we should have some sway in their decision."

Pat shook his head. "Tick tock, friend. We're nearing the twenty-fifth hour. But if you show them something soon, who knows."

Joe stood. "Well, you aren't my chain of command. So this goes two ways. One: you can help me. Two: you stay the fuck outta my way. Because the way I see it, I have until July fourth to clear out Baltimore."

"You're persistent, that much is true." Pat sloshed the scotch around his glass. "I'll give you some leeway in missions, so long as they stay heading toward Baltimore."

"Just do me a favor: No more need-to-know mission bullshit. I don't need the heartburn."

Pat swallowed the last of the scotch. "Aye aye. You have to give me a little leeway, too, there, shipmate. Nobody would have thought that my last mission would be *this*."

9

NINE

June 15

Riding one of the horses, Joe had Cara with him as they trotted around and laughed together. If not for the M4 slung over Joe's shoulder, you would have thought it was months ago, before the meaning of dead had changed.

It looked like any other sunny afternoon on the farm with the family. Joe's younger sister, Rachael, was in the other field jumping over a picnic table on her horse, Tuffy. Spencer sat on a fence watching. Out by the barn, Greg and Ted were feeding the chickens and collecting eggs.

As Joe turned and headed for the fence, Joe's mother Terry smiled and waved to him. Joe tried to return the smile, but it came out as a false grin and back to the emotionless look he'd worn since his wife passed. "Hi, Ma. How are things?"

"Things are things. You been up long?"

"Since five, I suppose. Fiddled around the barn until Cara came out."

Cara had her arms wrapped around Joe and her chin over his shoulder. "Dad, do you, like, have to go back out? We miss you."

Joe shook his head and frowned. "People's lives depend on it. I promise that if—that once things get back to normal, we'll take a vacation. You, me, Grammy. How about that island Aunt E and Uncle E are on?"

Grammy smiled. "I wouldn't mind seeing how the other half got along during all this mess."

Joe looked back at Cara. "Want to go for a ride?"

Cara smiled as she rolled her eyes and said, "Yeah, sure, Dad. That would be great." Cara hopped off the horse and opened the front gate. Joe walked the mare out through the gate where Cara jumped back on and they trotted down the road. As he rode toward the park, Joe pictured the neighborhood as it used to be. He galloped to the battery at Fort Smallwood Park, passing the plots of land the remaining neighbors, along with the guys from the VFW, had turned over and planted crops in the park. They were already starting to get some tomatoes and the corn was shooting up fast. Joe smiled when a couple waved as he and Cara rode by the playground. If not for the rifles and pistols it would have felt like a time not long past.

On the way out of the park Joe heard a sharp whistle.

He turned around and saw Tim as Cara waved. "Hey, bud," said Joe. "Enjoying your days off?"

Tim shot Joe a curious stare. "Sure, yeah. Kids were glad to see me and Christian. And I see you are actually taking some time as well. How about you youngin'? Enjoy hanging out with your Dad?"

Cara tilted her head a little. "It's okay I guess. Liked it better when he got time off and we could go somewhere fun. Would be great to go to the pool today, if that was still a thing."

Tim pointed down the road at the bay. "Big ass pool right there. Just convince him to take that rifle off."

Cara shuffled around on the back of the horse. "That would be great. Too bad I didn't get an invite on the boat yesterday."

Joe's shoulders rolled with his eyes as Cara finished talking.

"You hear about our next fishing trip?" asked Joe.

"Ha, I think everyone around here has heard about it. Once Pat's crew brings back the boats for tomorrow, I have to make up mounts for the 240s. I'm trying to get Dell and Spencer to help."

"Fine, I didn't want to help you anyway."

"Spend time with your family, my man." Tim shook his head. "But not gonna lie: Tomorrow night's mission sounds pretty sweet. Got a few tools already set aside for it."

Joe wondered what Tim had in mind. "Fair enough. Tomorrow then."

As they rode home, Joe felt Cara squeeze him tightly as they neared the farm. "Dad, I love you. Thanks for hanging out today."

Joe was stirred from his thoughts as she said it. "It was nice, Cara. Someday we'll get back to days where we lay on the couch, watch a terrible comedy. Eat something that leaves our fingers coated with orange cheese dust. I miss those days with you—and your mom." Joe fell silent and stared out at the Key Bridge as they rode past the water. He pictured the last time they were out on the boat. Joe swallowed hard and looked back at Cara. " I know I've been a bit distant lately, but it's just that—I don't know—everything feels so up in the air too often anymore."

Cara held onto him tighter. "Grammy says God is on our side."

Joe thought about his wife. He thought about the dead cannibals roaming the streets of Baltimore. Thought about how he wished he could shut his brain off, power down that voice in his head if only for a moment or two. "God is good," said Joe. "And we're with the good guys, right?"

"Mm. I guess." Cara rolled her shoulders and yawned. "But then like I wonder—why does a 'good' God allow stuff like children to be tortured and kidnapped. Or even like for murderers to go free?"

Joe blinked several times. He swallowed nothing. He turned to try and see Cara's face. Joe knew he had to say something. Recount the story of Job, if nothing else. Except when Joe opened his mouth, nothing came out.

Cara stared at him expressionless. He felt dizzy as he spoke. "I've had my doubts, like when my dad died. When your mother," Joe trailed off. "But the fact that we are still here and thriving in this shitbox world—I don't know. Sometimes ya just gotta take it on faith, buddy. Too many times He was there for me when no other explanation sufficed. Trust me, have faith and we will make it through this."

* * *

That night, after getting home from a meeting at the VFW, Joe and Alex sat at the table with Greg and Ted. "You know, guys," said Joe, "this is pretty brave of you. Dangerously so. You sure the few of you going will be enough?"

Greg said, "I'm with Ted on this, one hundred percent. Absolutely. It's a pretty big risk, but you do know your mother is worried sick, right? I'm pretty sure she has spent most of her time praying, since Cara told her about your plan."

"Well, if we don't do it, then who? Imagine seeing us from that building and we never came back. I'd feel pretty shitty if they starved to death waiting for help that isn't coming."

Alex patted Joe on the back. "Joe's right. If they don't go get them out of there, they're dead. Either from the air strike or the Zs."

Joe's face went blank. "I'd hate for Mom and you guys to be trapped somewhere and get hope only to have it never come. That kind of shit can kill you faster than starving."

"It sucks," said Alex, "but Joe and his team are their last hope."

"It's the right thing to do, no question." Ted smiled. "The best you can do whenever shit hits the fan is simply the right thing. Most won't, but I'm proud of you guys for leading the way."

Joe snorted. "Careful there, Gramps. You wouldn't want people to think you give compliments."

"I'd hate for the last thing I said to you before you left was how much of a dumbass you were."

Greg's face shifted from happy to solemn. "We both support what you guys are doing. And if you need anything, we're here. Just don't do this to make up for things you had no control of."

"Ain't about that." Joe shook his head. "I'm simply doing what everyone else should be."

"A lot of us are doing the best we can with what we have."

Joe nodded at Greg. "You are doing more than enough. I haven't worried once about the girls knowing you two are watching things down here. Seriously. As for me I'm not up for discussion about it. It's gotta get done, so we're gonna do it."

On his way to his room, Joe saw Cara leaning in the corner of the hallway waiting for him. He winked at her. "Pulling an all nighter?"

Cara looked grim. "Can we talk?"

"Of course." Joe walked into his room. "Shoot."

Cara whispered, "I'm worried about you." A tear ran down her cheek and clung to her chin. Joe wiped it away, then wrapped his arms around her and squeezed. Tears flowed steadily now and Cara sobbed. "Can't someone else go?"

Joe choked back a little before answering. "No, buddy, no one else would go. My idea, my job."

Cara shoved him away. "Isn't one dead parent *enough*?"

"I will be back tomorrow," said Joe. "All of us will."

Cara faked smile. "Heroes are in battlefields and cemeteries, and every moment that makes a hero was a tragedy until *no one* survived to tell the tale." Cara shook her head. "To me it sounds like a bunch of dead people who we make up stories to help us feel better about their stupidity."

Joe stepped toward Cara and reached for her. She backed away, telling him don't and then turned and ran.

Joe followed her to her bedroom. When Cara looked up the tears continued to flow but she was quiet. Joe didn't know exactly what to say. He looked around her room. Atop her dresser stood framed pictures of family and friends. A shark tooth necklace they had picked out on their trip to Saint Thomas sat on top of an old photo album. Joe knelt down in front of Cara. "I'm gonna be straight with you, you deserve that. I have to go tomorrow and rescue those people because no one else will step up. When I saw them, all I could picture was you and your mother, Grammy and Pop. I will come back to ya bud, promise. Whether it means marching through Hell or high water."

Cara wiped her eyes and hugged him. "I'm sorry, Dad. I love you. It just sucks seeing all those guys play it safe, while all my people risk everything."

Joe kissed her on the forehead. "I love you. Try and get some sleep."

Joe walked out and headed to his room trying to get the conversation out of his head.

He laid in bed for hours, unable to sleep. The stress eventually broke him and he felt tears running down his cheek and neck.

10

TEN

June 16

Following the morning briefing at the VFW, Joe had his team meet at the farm to run mockups of the night's mission. It wasn't precise, but after a few runs they found their rhythm.

Joe, Dell, and Tim dressed in Carhartt overalls, thick work shirts, and steel-toed boots. Sean, Ryan, and James wore fatigues—Marines for Ryan, Army for Sean and James.

"This shit's going to give me heat stroke," said Tim after the fourth drill.

"You'd rather be bit?" Joe said. "Two more, then it's onto the boats and we'll load up."

As they finished up the last drill, Joe saw Greg wave to them holding a plate of food. Tim tore off the heavy Carhartt shirt and sprinted to the door with Dell right behind him. As the rest of them walked ahead, Joe squinted at the sun as it was starting to touch the roof of the house. The breeze was steady at Joe's back which bode well for the ride into the harbor.

While Joe went over the last details in his head, Ryan ran back and said, "Come on fuckface, let's go eat before Tim and Dell get everything. It's easier to worry on a full stomach."

After dinner, Joe and his team headed to the pier at the park where Pat's guys had left the boats the prior night. Everyone was there when they pulled up, including Alex and Pat. They were loading ammo, water, food, and first aid supplies into the boats. Alex fought to get a grip on the bigger items. His arm swung wildly as the muscle memory still had him trying to reach for a grip with the missing hand and forearm. His face showed teeth with a flat expression. Joe knew that look. He'd seen it a thousand times before from his childhood. As Joe went to help, Alex politely said through clenched teeth, "I'm fine, grab something else."

Joe put his hands up in surrender and walked to Dell's boat to start putting away the supplies.

Pat set a heavy cooler at Joe's feet. "Open her when it's over, not a moment before."

Joe nodded and swung the cooler in the boat's forward cabin. Once the cabin was loaded, Joe climbed out back onto the pier where the rest of the team had gathered.

Joe sat on one of the pilings and addressed the group. "Everyone that leaves here with me tonight, I want to thank you. We are the only hope these folks got, and we are the only ones that got the balls to do this. So I say fuck it, let's go do some hero shit since no one else will."

Dell climbed down and fired up the old diesel as the rest of the team climbed into their boats. As they made their way to the harbor, Joe closed his eyes and tried to think if he had forgotten anything. He came up with nothing, leaned against the transom and closed his eyes one last time, even though he wouldn't be able to sleep.

As they sat in the harbor, the last of the day's light began to fade. The boats were all in position and Jimmy's group was frantically scurrying around the back deck. Joe gave the go ahead to start engaging the Zs and it drew a crowd quickly. They had figured out that piling up the Zs and then shooting one or two worked wonders for drawing them in.

Once the Zs became so packed that they couldn't move, Sarge and Matt opened up the 240s. Pieces of Zs were flying and hitting the ones behind them as the rounds passed through hitting multiple targets. One Z Joe was watching got hit in the head. Pieces of its skull hit the one behind it in the face, blinding it, and causing it to stumble forward and fall into the harbor. They were making a bloody mess. For every Z they shot, it seemed like another immediately replaced it. *They just kept on coming. Relentless. It reminded Joe of something Tim told him once, that there was a fine line between stupidity and bravery.*

As the moon started to climb, Joe radioed, "Jimmy, you guys are doing great. Thirty mikes and we're gonna hit the hill. Should be about fifty rounds in that box with the flare gun. Use them often enough to get their attention, but don't waste 'em."

A flare went sailing over the square followed by a long rip from the 240 before Joe heard Jimmy respond, "Roger that."

Time was up. Spencer pulled the boat alongside the pier by the Rusty Anchor Restaurant and waited for everyone to offload. The pier jutted out from the restaurant on the south side of the harbor, the closest pier to Federal Hill, and farthest from Jimmy's deadrise, which was busy making a distraction.

Joe turned to Spencer. "Keep her running. Shouldn't be too long."

They passed the two-story waterfront restaurant and approached a parking garage a few blocks south. Up ahead, Ryan signaled for everyone to get down. As the team hit their knees, a pair of Zs came into view. Both were stocky and moving slowly. Joe could smell them. They reeked like a fish house dumpster. Joe prayed there weren't more behind them. The Zs shuffled toward the red flares and loud gunshots from Jimmy's team. Once they passed, Ryan waved for Joe's group to take the corner of the parking garage.

Joe's team ran forward and kneeled to position. Dell watched Ryan's team advance, while Tim watched the corner and Joe eyed the area facing away from the structure.

Tim leaned back and whispered, "Two more coming. Must be couples' night."

"How close will they get?"

"Close. Too close."

Joe slung his rifle and pulled the Kabar. "Let's do this, then break for the top of the hill."

The Zs remained focused on the flares, so they unknowingly passed Joe and his team. Tim checked the corner and signaled all clear. Joe and Dell quickly crept up behind them. Joe lunged forward, rammed the Kabar into the nape of the zombie's neck. The squelch of the knife into its soft flesh and the thud when it hit the ground caused the other Z to turn and face them. Dell swung a machete into its throat, lodging it into its carotid artery, and sent blood spraying out. Dell, wide-eyed, kicked the back of its knees and heard the snap of bones. As it hit the ground, blood was still squirting from its neck. Dell checked his clothes for blood, finding a dime-sized amount on his shirt and a hundred flecks on his shirt sleeve. Dell wiped the sweat from his eyes, then bent over and wiped his hands on his thighs. When he looked up, he saw Joe staring. Dell gave him a crooked smile and thumbs up.

Joe's legs burned as he trudged up the grassy Federal Hill Park. Though it's only about a forty foot climb, it felt like a thousand.

Near the top, Joe paused to admire the large American flag flapping lazily in the breeze. The flag's ends were frayed and an amorphic brown stain marred the two lowest white and red stripes. Still, it was a thing of beauty.

They crested the hill and Joe signaled a stop at the flagpole. The group fanned out and caught their breath. James whispered, "Small group of company, far side of the park."

"Let's take the house on the corner," said Joe. "Best to let them pass than be forced to engage them."

At the park's corner, they stopped to check the road. Sean whispered clear and they crossed the road to the house where they saw two guys waving an American flag from the roof. Joe covered the door and waved Ryan over. Tim and Dell covered the street. Ryan's team made it to the front door. Ryan knocked to the tune, "Shave and a haircut." Two knocks came from the other side of the door before it swung open.

Ryan greeted the stoutly built man who answered the door. "Two days ago, you saw us in the harbor. We're here to extract you and your people."

The man smiled, backing up to let them in. Ryan's team entered then came back out the door and waved Joe's team in. Joe's team darted across the street and in through the front door. Once inside, Joe signaled Ryan's team to spread out, just in case. Joe caught a strong whiff of bleach as he passed the bathroom and looked in to see a bucket next to a stack of old Baltimore

Sun newspapers.

After he scanned the room again, Joe introduced himself to the large man. He had a bald head, dark eyes, and the build of a former NFL linebacker. He said his name was Colton Simms, and that the other man they'd seen on the roof was his brother, Reese, who was seated on a beige loveseat, his right arm slung along its back and left arm cocked on the armrest. Reese was a slender version of his brother, though had the same dark eyes. The brothers appeared friendly and relieved to see new, human faces. They wanted to know where Joe and Ryan were going, and when they were leaving.

"We have a boat waiting and plan to load you guys up in ten mikes," Joe said. "Grab any gear you can hike with and any and all weapons you can carry."

The brothers hustled upstairs to get their stuff. A few minutes later they came down the stairs with duffle bags and padded weapons cases. Joe noticed a tattoo of a parachute wrapped in silver wings on Colton's forearm.

"You were Army?" asked Joe.

"Yeah," said Colton. He flicked his head to the side at Reese. "Both of us were 82nd Airborne out of Bragg."

Sean asked, "Rangers?"

"Nah," Reese said. "Regular old grunts."

Joe cocked his head. "Tell me how two grunts get up here with several guns and no communications?"

"We came to visit." Colton smiled. "Brought the guns because we were going to take my little cousin shooting. Stayed here with a friend from school. But when things got bad, our friend wanted to make a break." Colton smacked his forearm and glanced at the flattened mosquito and blood streak before wiping it over the belly of his shirt. "We tried to convince him to stay, but fear got the best of him. Fortunately, he left a lot of food and water, so we hunkered down."

"Got to cut this short, guys. Don't want the boat ditching us," said Sean. "Let's double-time."

"Back door into the alley would be best," Colton said. "From there, it's maybe a quarter-mile to the dock."

"Good," Joe said.

Colton and Reese walked to the back door where Joe stopped them. "Guys, real quick—don't shoot unless they're close and you've got no other choice. Mouse-fart quiet is the name of the game." Joe twirled his index finger and wrist in the air. "Roll out."

The alley smelled of shit and its only tenants were a few large rats.

Once the men made it down the alley to the park, Joe winked at Ryan. "Let's go."

The men sprinted across the road, into the waterfront park. Joe called to Spencer for extract when he heard a shot. He looked over and saw a dead Z to his right. His heart now thumping hard, Joe willed his legs faster as he crossed the street into Rash Field.

Closing in on the pier, the men saw a dozen zombies shuffling around the bend. Out in front, Sean and James raised their guns and began firing. They succeeded in stopping two of them, but the others steadily gained ground.

Tim radioed, "Cut a path, got more coming at our—" The sound of Ryan's 249 cut Tim off as he fired uphill at a pack of Zs racing toward them.

Joe yelled into the mic, "On me, move!" He charged forward at the pack, spraying bullets. Joe dropped a mag and was attempting to reload as he jogged when he noticed the closest Z was within lunging range. Joe let the rifle fall to his side on its sling as he kicked the Z's chest, sending it onto its back and giving Joe time to pull his Glock and fire four bullets into its chest. The other Zs from the pack fell as Joe's team fanned out and unloaded their mags.

Once the men passed the pier gate, Joe stopped and slammed it shut. Joe knew the latch wouldn't hold for long, but it would buy them some time. As they sprinted down the pier, Joe yelled, "Load the boat and meet us at the end of the dock. Tim, come with me."

Joe ran past Spencer and their boat to the end of the dock and jumped on a sixty-five-foot Hatteras motor yacht that was tied off to the edge of the dock. Following close behind, Tim asked, "We trying to steal this thing?"

"Let's pull it away from the pier, drop anchor, burn it down."

"We should've brought marshmallows."

"The light should help draw 'em away from the high rise."

"Damn, you're serious," said Tim. "I'm gonna hate myself for this."

"Get her pushed off the dock and lit up. I'll send her off." Joe said, "You go in the engine room and kill the fire suppression."

Dell pulled up alongside the bow of the yacht. He had a wet hand towel draped over his head and down his neck. The back of his shirt looked drenched. "The fuck you two doing?"

Joe tossed him a line. "Drag her over by the Science Center."

The Maryland Science Center sat on the southwest corner of the harbor. Joe hoped that the museum's stories of glass that faced the fire would amplify the brightness of the flames, drawing all nearby Zs toward it.

Dell hooked up the line and towed the boat slowly toward the Science Center.

Tim emerged from the yacht's engine compartment. He had disabled the fire arresting system and was carrying two fuel cans and a gallon of motor oil. He dowsed the furniture and teak deck then hopped onto Dell's boat and scrambled into the cabin. Tim brought out the flare gun and gave it to Joe.

Tim cut the line to Dell's boat and told Joe, "Fire it up!"

Dell spun the wheel, headed to the opposite side of the harbor. Joe raised the flare gun and fired it into the yacht. Moments later, the yacht began burning, illuminating the entire harbor. The zombies snarled and ran toward it like moths.

Joe radioed Jimmy, "How you on ammo?"

"Getting low. Barely have enough to keep their attention. Definitely won't have enough for a firefight. Want us to shift toward that campfire to try and give you more space for the high rise?"

"Yes, a little. We'll be overboard in fifteen. Gonna give it a bit longer to grab their full attention."

"Gotcha. We'll slow down and move 'em toward the Science Center. Stay frosty, brother."

Dell handed the helm to Spencer as he pulled up to a small dock hidden between the Aquarium and the Baltimore Trade Center. The team disembarked at the dock, ran across Pratt street, and made it to the first building. They caught their breath before heading one more block north and two blocks west to the T. Rowe Price building where a thick sliding glass door marked the entrance.

Tim pulled a small crowbar from his pack and edged the door open.

They ran past the elevators. After searching two different hallways, they found a stairwell. They ran up to the third floor. Joe yanked on the door several times. It wouldn't budge. He kicked it in frustration.

Through the small window in the door, they saw a rope tied to the handle. Joe signaled for Tim to break the window. Tim slammed a center punch into the glass, then reached through the glass and cut the rope with his knife.

Joe opened the door and the men fanned out. "Don't be alarmed," Joe said. "We're here to get everyone to safety."

A few seconds of silence passed before a shadowed figure came around the corner with hands raised.

Joe walked slowly toward the man. "Buddy, you okay?"

The man was middle-aged and overweight, dressed in a half-buttoned up Oxford with the sleeves rolled above his forearms. His navy dress slacks had a long tear from his right inner thigh up to his crotch. His eyes weren't fully open.

"We have boats on standby," said Joe. "How many others besides you?"

"Used to be forty. At least forty." The man stared down at the curly hairs peeking out from the top of his shirt. He began buttoning up, saying, "Now? Now I'd say twenty-three, twenty-two."

"Get them," Joe said.

The man shuffled away.

Tim looked over at Joe and Dell. "That fucker had a hard time. Bet it sucked being stuck up here."

Dell wiped the sweat from his brow. "Yeah, buddy, we definitely had it better than them."

Joe hushed the two as he saw the man return with an assortment of desperate looking people—all adults, all clearly terrified.

"Ladies and gentlemen," Joe said, "we are here to help move you into safer territory."

One man's hand shot up. "You from the government?"

"I wouldn't say that, no. Now, nobody has to, but I urge you to come with us."

The people in the crowd were looking at each other and mumbling.

Joe whistled to Dell and Tim. "Guys, take point. We're moving. Ryan, your guys take the rear." Joe raised his voice to the crowd, saying, "We're running low on time. Follow me."

As they marched down the steps with the crowd of people following, Joe's anxiety caused him to stop and look back. To his surprise they were all moving calmly and in a single file line.

At the front door, they formed up again. Joe instructed them to get in groups of three and stick together. "Stay against the walls and don't run off on your own, if you want to live." Joe said, "You see any Zs, don't scream, don't yell, and damn sure don't move. You will get to the boat as long as you follow these directions." Joe swung his hand in the air, motioning for them to follow.

The street appeared empty. They made it to the corner of the mall before they spotted a Z. The group crouched down against the wall and waited. Gun shots from the harbor caught the Z's attention and it ran off.

Joe stood and signaled. They made it to Pratt Street, but once there came upon a large group of nearly fifty Zs. Joe keyed the radio and told Ryan to come to the front with Sean and James to keep watch on the herd.

Joe signaled and told everyone to form a big circle. "Here's the deal. The zombies have poor vision. So, we are gonna walk across the street like we own it. But don't look up, just look ahead. If they make us, we'll eliminate them. But I need you all to stay together. If it comes to it, I'd rather have you run 500 yards to the boats, not a half mile."

Joe walked to Ryan and told him that his team takes the lead, that if the Zs attack, open up the 240. Sean and James were to back Ryan up, whereas Tim and Dell were to watch Joe.

As the group got to the other side of Pratt Street near the boats, a heavyset middle-aged woman began to shake and stopped moving. The businessman Joe had met earlier held her hand and tried to calm her, but she ripped her hand away and bolted toward the boat. The sudden movement alerted the Zs and they charged in her direction.

Joe radioed, "Hot extract, hot extract! Bring in the three boats and load the pier. Shoot everything that tails us! We've got twenty-eight total: six team, twenty-two refugees. Spencer, get the boys up there and aim for oncoming stragglers from your east. Be rounding corner of the Trade Center momentarily."

As Joe looked to their boat, he saw Spencer and Christian perched on the boat's roof. They opened fire into the crowd of Zs. Colton and Reese were positioned below them and fired as well.

Joe turned the corner of the Trade Center and grabbed Ryan's shoulder. "Let her eat!"

Ryan raised the barrel on the M249 and cut down a portion the zombie horde. Sean and James had taken position and watched Ryan's back as they walked and fired. Out front, Tim and Dell fired off the hip as they led the group to the boats.

Joe caught up to the panicked woman, who was crouched in a bush, just past the Trade Center, 100 yards from the dock. "Get up and move your ass unless you want to fucking die here." He grabbed the woman under her arm and yanked her upright. The businessman followed behind Joe, took her other arm, and helped Joe drag her toward the boats, which now waited backed up against the small floating dock. As they got close, Joe nudged them toward the boat, then turned and raced back toward Ryan.

Joe fell back to a point against the Trade Center, working his way to Sean and James. "People are at the boat, move!" Sean took off and Joe drew his pistol, firing over his shoulder at a Z that appeared at the edge of the building. Joe hit the Z in its gut. Undeterred, the Z charged for Sean. Joe emptied his magazine into its side. Sean turned and struck the zombie in the forehead with the gunstock, knocking it to the ground. Joe yelled, "Go! Move it!"

Sean sprinted alongside Ryan, but James held fast and continued to fire. The Zs were within ten yards when Joe told James to go.

Joe stood up, ran another twenty-five yards to the pier entrance and emptied another mag. He turned and witnessed the first zombie slam into

James, sinking its teeth into his left shoulder. James tried to shake him off, but it was too late. James vanished under a mob of Zs.

Joe sprinted toward the boat.

At the dock, Joe pulled out a grenade and threw it over the bushes near the Trade Center. He jumped in the boat and yelled, "Down! Nade out!" The blast echoed off the building as they pulled away.

Joe picked himself up from the deck.

"Jay?" Sean asked.

Joe stared at the ground and shook his head.

Tears welled in Sean's eyes. He dragged the heels of his palms across his eyes. Sean blinked fast, saying, "Fucking allergies."

Joe looked at the group they'd rescued. "That woman who broke out and ran, it cost us a good man."

"A *fucking* good man," said Sean.

"A fucking good man," said Joe.

Sean inhaled deeply before letting the air out. "Til Valhalla, brother."

Joe went into Dell's cabin, pulled his earpiece out, and took off his gear. He remembered and saw the cooler Pat had brought him before they left. Joe opened it. Inside was a box of cigars and a twelve-pack of beer on ice. On top was a small plastic bag with a piece of paper inside. Joe lit one of the cigars and grabbed the piece of paper.

Joe,

If you're reading this, you survived, which is a great relief to all of us. By this time, you're probably thinking about what went wrong, why it went wrong, and how you could've fixed it. Don't. Cherish a win. A win's a win. Pass the beers and cigars out to your men and congratulate them, no matter the imperfections of the outcome.

We'll talk soon.

Best,

Pat

11

ELEVEN

June 17

Pat and Alex were on Dell's pier when the boats pulled in. Dell kept his boat in the cove until the rescuees had been offloaded.

When Dell pulled to the pier, Pat climbed aboard.

Pat asked Sean, "Can we talk?"

Sean nodded.

Pat smiled. "I'll give you a ride."

Before Joe climbed off he noticed gloom in Dell's eyes. "Ryan, go on ahead. I'll be up in a minute."

As Ryan walked to the truck, Joe said to Dell, "Level with me, bro. You good?"

Dell's hands trembled a bit. "I, I—I'm good. Just that close call with the Z. That's all."

Joe exhaled, feeling the last bit of energy leave him. "This new world is taking some getting used to."

"How does anyone get used to this?" Dell wiped sweat from his forehead. "Anyway, been a rough night. You best get some sleep."

The boards creaked underfoot as Joe walked up the pier. He turned back and saw Dell drinking from the bottle of Southern Comfort he kept under the console.

Once inside the truck, Joe turned the key and the truck rumbled to life. He sat back and lit a cigarette. "Glad you're okay."

Ryan said, "Shit, man. Better than okay. Who doesn't love dodging rabid corpses on the daily?"

Joe blew a gray cloud out his window and put the truck in drive. "Definitely. Right up there with wrestling grizzly bears."

After Joe and Ryan had made it home to the farm, Ryan said, "Bro, there's something else."

Joe shifted his body and relaxed his left arm on the windowsill. "You going to make me guess?"

"That shit was not your fault. Hope you know that."

Joe stared out the windshield. He pointed to a small crack near the top corner. "I was driving the beltway when this eighteen-wheeler—this was a Tuesday or some shit, one day after I got off work, I don't know—and this eighteen-wheeler kicked up a rock, a few of them actually. Whatever, it left that crack."

"Look fuckwit, if you get told to move and don't, that shit's on you. You know that shit. Ain't your fucking fault he died."

Ryan stared at Joe who was still looking at the crack in the windshield.

"Maybe I was driving to close," said Joe. "I mean, there's three lanes, isn't there?"

Ryan exited the truck and slammed the door. He turned back as he walked toward the house, hands cupped around his mouth, he yelled, "Don't be a martyr, Joe. Your kid deserves better."

Joe stuck his left hand out the window, middle finger raised.

"You too, brother," said Ryan. "You too."

Joe got out and sat on the tailgate. He pulled one of the cigars from his pocket and ran it slowly under his nose, smelling it. He held the cigar at both ends and rolled it back and forth. "Goddamnit, James."

A while later, after he had finished the cigar, Joe went inside the house and found Cara seated at the table. As he walked up behind her, Cara's head whipped around. She locked eyes with him before kicking her chair away and charging him. She slapped him hard at the waist then wrapped him in a hug.

ELEVEN

***

The next morning, the VFW parking lot was full. Inside, people periodically looked at Joe. A few had been crying.

Ryan walked over and squeezed Joe's bicep. "Bad news travels fast."

"Hm. Right."

Joe found Pat and Alex at their usual spot, perched on two barstools, their backs to him. They were hunched over a laptop. Pat glanced over his shoulder as Joe approached.

"Well," said Joe, "when's the next deployment? Must be thousands in Baltimore running out of food."

"I have two crews out clearing up to the city line," said Pat.

"Doesn't answer my question."

"I don't have a timeline for it, at the moment."

"Okay, okay," said Joe. "You understand that people starve, then they die. They die, then they're slurping out your fucking brains. You get it?"

"Roger that, soldier, I get it. I do. But I also get that hasty decisions are the fastest way to lose more people."

Joe's chest raised as he inhaled and held his breath.

"Sorry, I didn't mean it like that. I wasn't implying anything."

Joe bit slightly into his bottom lip and held his hands up above his shoulders, backing away.

"Joe, come on. That's not what I meant."

Joe walked into the hall. People encircled his guys, at least the ones he saw. Some people were hugging them and shaking their hands. Joe beelined for the door. Last thing he needed was conversation with strangers.

As Joe reached for the door, a woman said, "Sir. Sir. Excuse me, sir." She was younger than Joe, and had long, dark hair, and brown eyes. "I wanted to thank you."

Joe shook his head. "Sorry, I don't—have we met?"

She smiled. "Your team pulled us out of the city last night. We saw you leave the first day and then come back and shoot all those—those hideous things. Thank you. I can't say it enough. Thank you, thank you, thank you."

97

She wrapped her arms around Joe and hugged him.

"It's no problem. Really."

Joe walked out to his truck and grabbed a cigar from the console. He lit it, then took a seat on his tailgate. As he puffed on the cigar, Alex came out and sat next to him. Alex didn't speak. He just occasionally swung his legs.

Sun in his eyes, Joe squinted as he held the cigar in his teeth. "I'm not a mind reader." Joe pulled the cigar out and studied it. "Spit it out."

Alex scooted back a little. "Thought you could use some company."

Joe puffed the cigar and blew out smoke. "Yeah, I bet. You seen Dell?"

"He came in earlier, wasn't feeling good. Left after seeing the doc."

Joe laid back into the truck bed. "Too many people in there. I swear the room got smaller somehow."

"You think that's bad. Imagine being reduced to only one jerk off hand. You can't scan porn with just one hand. I'm telling you."

Joe laughed and Alex smiled.

Alex rubbed his cheek and said, "Keep in mind they're going to expect you to speak when they start James' funeral."

Joe felt a heavy weight swell inside his chest. "Right. The funeral."

As Alex walked away Joe put up the tailgate and climbed into the cab of the truck. He fired up the old diesel engine, dropped the seat back and pulled his old hat over his eyes as he thought about what to say. *What coulda been done so he wouldn't have died? How should we do it better next time? The hell am I gonna say in front of all these people?* Joe's mind raced. Feeling his eyes get heavy, he turned off the truck and resigned himself to a quick nap.

When Joe woke up to the sound of another truck, he realized that his quick nap was closer to two hours. He wiped the sleep from his eyes and went back inside and sat down with everyone to eat.

After the meal, Pat stood at the small podium at the front of the room. He cleared his throat and swallowed. "I would like to thank everyone who helped prepare this—well—this feast." Pat smiled and rubbed his stomach. "Every one of you have played an important role in getting us here. In surviving. Guys like Doctor Jeff and Phil. Those guys have been working tirelessly taking care of our health and overseeing that we get electric back in our houses.

"Some of you have been behind the scenes taking inventory of the stores we have brought in and making sure we know what we need to look for as we venture out into this new reality we find ourselves living in. Others have used their intuition and initiative to further the ground that we hold. We're talking about hours upon hours worked, making things happen when most would have given up.

"But all these things come at a cost. As most of you know, last night we lost a man during a rescue mission. We have all lost people to this plague, but he was the first casualty we have suffered on mission since we united to fight the zombies. This is a sad day, and it reminds us of war's ultimate price: blood.

"I ask that all of you forever remember Private First Class Phillip Andrew James, or James as most you knew him." Pat raised his bottle and the whole room followed suit. "May Charon grant you passage across the river to whatever Heaven it is you seek." Pat nodded and said, "To James."

The whole room said, "To James!"

After taking a drink, Pat said that if anyone had something to say, now was the time.

Sean stood and walked to the podium. Pat gently tapped Sean's shoulder with the fat of his fist and left him.

"James," said Sean, "he was my friend. He loved the mission. Loved the group we ran with. If his family were here with us, I'm sure they'd be proud of the man he was. I'm going to miss him." Sean choked the edges of the podium, knuckles turning white. "The next hundred kills I take against this godforsaken enemy, I dedicate to his memory."

Sean punched the podium top once, then returned to his seat where he grabbed his beer and guzzled it. He set the beer on his table and sucked at the suds clinging to his beard.

Following Sean, several others used the time to share their memories of James.

One of them was an older Veteran, Jim Shaw, who said that when he first met James, he had been through hell making it here but still wanted to do everything to make it easier on us old guys. "He would stick around here after his guys had went out all day and still try and help us keep the hall squared away. Not only did he work his ass off, but he was always telling us how 'Joe did it.' Or how his team got it done after asking me and some of the other guys what they would do. It killed me to hear that he paid the price for rescuing all these good people and I hope somewhere in Heaven he is smiling at us as he sits with his mom and dad." Jim Shaw said, "To James!"

As Jim stepped down, a woman Joe didn't recognize walked up. She had dark red hair and bright blue eyes. Joe couldn't place her as she took the podium. "Hello," she said. "My name is Dana Banner. I was one of the people trapped in that office building when James and the others came for us. As we were getting ready to cross the road where we saw all the Zs, I felt paralyzed and couldn't control my shivering. James put his arm around me and whispered to me, 'Don't worry miss, I won't let any of 'em get to you. We're almost there.'"

Dana stopped and wiped her eyes. As she collected herself she looked back at the crowd and said, "Because of him and his friends we are alive today and I—I just wanted to thank him and all of you. We had lost hope. But thanks to him and all of you we got it back. Thank you."

As she walked away Joe watched Tim smile and wave his head signaling Joe to the podium. Joe sat there feeling very small. After all the thoughts and speeches, he didn't know what to add.

When the podium had been vacant for a minute, Tim pushed on Joe's shoulder until Joe nearly fell out of his seat. "Batter up."

Bottle in hand, Joe took the podium and blinked. Everything looked blurry. He blinked again and sniffed. "I, uh, well. James. James, man, where do I begin?" Joe tilted his beer to his lips and drank. Finished, he wiped his arm across his mouth. "I'm not really big on speeches. And by that I mean I'm terrible at them." Joe blinked again, then went to take another drink, but his bottle was empty. He shook the beer over his mouth, got down the last drops. "James was a good guy. He was—always ready for the mission, no matter how absurd it was. He was always up for it. As Sean would say, James had giant balls."

Sean pounded his table twice, rattling the dishes and silverware. "Giant fucking balls, man. Giant. Had to hold them or else they'd drag on the ground."

Several men in the crowd laughed and smiled.

Joe picked at the corner of the label on his beer bottle. "He never complained. Never argued over dumb little bullshit. He was a good soldier. My regret is that I won't get another chance to know him better."

That night after dinner, Joe heard Tim's diesel pull into the driveway. As Joe walked out, he saw Dell in the passenger seat, windows rolled up and his forehead inches from the AC vents which were on full blast.

Tim came around the front of the truck. He wouldn't look directly at Joe. Tim had bloodshot, red-rimmed eyes. With his lips parted and shaped in an O, he exhaled slowly. "Brother, I've got shit news. Like real shit. Like real fucked up shit. It'd be best if Ryan, Spencer, and Alex were here for it, too. But only them."

Inside the truck, Dell struggled to pull his sweaty t-shirt off. Joe cocked his head, then shifted his sights back to Tim. "All right."

After Joe had Ryan, Spencer, and Alex in tow, Tim told them to get in the back. They needed to go for a ride.

The men filled the bed of the old white F-250. Alex took the corner of the truck and pushed his foot against the wheel tub, saying, "What's good?"

Joe flicked his head toward the passenger seat, where a shirtless Dell sat leaned over, his cheek against the dashboard. "Take a guess."

Alex squinted into the dusty rear panel.

When they reached Tim's house, Tim climbed out of the truck and walked into his garage where a picnic table was in the now empty bay. Joe saw pistols on the table next to a bottle of Southern Comfort. Joe felt paralyzed at first when he looked toward the passenger door.

Joe knew.

He dug deep and found the courage to jump out of the truck and make his way to the passenger door where Dell was slowly climbing down.

Dell swatted at Joe and lowered his ass to the concrete. He leaned back on two hands. Buried in the black hair on his chest lay a gold cross on a tarnished silver chain. It was the first time Joe had ever seen Dell wear jewelry.

Dell forced a smile.

All Joe could think to say was, "Dude."

Dell swatted at Joe again, saying, "Shit happens."

Joe helped Dell to his feet and followed him to the picnic table. Dell breathed heavily while he poured drinks. Once everyone had two fingers of SoCo, he pulled an unmarked blue bottle out and shook two pills in his mouth. He swallowed them dry, emptied his glass, then sat at the table.

Everyone was on edge when Dell spoke. "No easy way to say this so I'm gonna just be blunt. That fucker last night got me. I mean he didn't bite me, but some of the blood got on my hands, and, and when I wiped my eyes—well, fuck. Do the math."

A tear streamed down Dell's cheek. "Got confirmation this morning—from the doc. Says I probably have about twenty-four hours before I—before I lose myself to this shit."

Tim's eyes started to swell from wiping them.

"Hang on," said Joe. "We're missing something. There has to be a way to slow it or even—."

Dell put his hand up. "Don't want any bitch tears. Don't want a pity party."

"Pat probably knows of medicine the Feds have."

"Joe, there's nothing they can do. I talked to Pat after getting the death sentence from the Doc."

"Not like it'd be the first time he lied, Dell. Let me talk to him."

"No, man. Be cool. Just be cool."

"He fucking owes us," said Joe, "far as I'm concerned."

"Shut up. Shut up. Shut the fuck up." Dell breathed so hard now his chest was visibly rising and falling. "We do this my way, end of story. I love you, Joe, but you're wrong. There's no cure. No chemotherapy for this shit. Death or death are the only options here. All right?"

Joe crossed his arms over his chest and exhaled. "Okay, bro. Loud and clear. I hear you."

Dell leaned forward on his elbows. "To explain my absence, he's gonna tell everyone that I fell and broke my leg. Jeff will run my boat for the upcoming missions. I don't want anyone foggy when they go into Baltimore."

Joe felt woozy, his knees weak. He sat down. "What about Ashley and the kids?"

"Already said goodbye. We spent the morning together. They know I'm not coming home tonight."

Alex said, "How so? You got twenty-four hours, according to the Doc."

"I saved the fun part for you guys," said Dell, with a lopsided smile. He grabbed a handgun. Barrel pointed downward at the picnic table, he held its brown grip lazily with two fingers and shook it.

Joe counted all the pistols. "You can't possibly be serious."

Dell slammed his hand on the picnic table. "You'd rather me, what? Does someone here want to offer me a couch for the night? Because I sure as fuck am not risking my family's life."

Spencer stood. "I'll do it. You'd do the same for me."

Dell nodded slowly, saying, "My man. Good." Dell looked around the table. Everyone remained silent and avoided eye contact. "You guys gotta understand. Possibly it's nothing, but I don't wanna risk it. Who knows, yeah? I've never died before." Dell tilted his head back and stared at a rusty shovel hanging on the wall. He swallowed. He took deep breaths. His chest hair glistened with sweat. "If I *did* do it myself, though, man—and all that suicide shit's true—I'm fucked, because that's an elevator drop straight to Hell."

Joe felt tears welling up, blurring his vision. Once that first one ran down his cheek, he picked up his glass and swallowed it down. The liqueur burned in his stomach.

"The silence is deafening, guys," said Dell. "But I do intend to finish that bottle, regardless. And the least you dickheads can do is not let me drink alone. Except you Spence," said Dell as he winked at Spencer. "You're one-hundred percent not a dickheads."

"You're joking about this? Absolutely insane. I need a cigarette," said Joe. He pulled out a softpack, lipped one straight out. The cigarette rested at the corner of his mouth, unlit. "*So,* five pistols, five of us. Bit much, don't you think?" Joe struck a match and lit his cigarette.

Dell swiped his forearm across his head, removing sweat. "I put blanks in four of them. This way no guilt. Easy peasy." Dell tried to smile, but it was crooked and full of dread. He grabbed the Southern Comfort bottle and held it his palm. He examined the label, then screwed the top off. "Once I finish her, I want you guys to aim for my chest. Lemon squeezy."

Ryan glanced at the pistols before asking Dell if it wouldn't be better to swallow a whole bunch of pills and fall asleep while taking a bath.

Dell poured another glass from the bottle. "Chest shots would be best. The old lady says she'd like to see me one last time."

Tim grabbed the glass. "Okay, time to drink. Dell is a warrior and we will send him off as he wishes." Tim threw back the glass and inhaled deeply before he swallowed.

The next few hours the men sat around talking about old times and trying their best to laugh as they normally would. Joe tried to drink away the thought of what they were going to have to do when the bottle ran out.

After Dell poured and downed his last drink, he picked up the first pistol and handed it to Spencer. As he handed Spencer the pistol, Joe saw him whisper something into his ear before he let go of the embrace. Dell repeated this act with Alex, Tim, and Ryan. Joe swallowed the last of his glass and raised himself to go and do his duty.

Walking to Dell, Joe's legs were concrete. There, he took the pistol and pulled the slide just enough to see the brass. He wrapped his arms around Dell and felt his chest jump as held back tears. Joe told him, "I'm sorry, brother. I'm so sorry."

Dell squeezed him tightly and whispered, "Keep an eye on my family. And don't stop shooting 'til they're dead. Really dead. All of them. And between you and me, your gun has a blank." Dell let go and stepped back. "Love you, bud. See you on the other side."

Tim came over, wrapped his arm around Dell's waist and helped him out onto the dirtmound where Dell slumped over and tried to hold himself up. Pistol in hand, Joe gathered with the others. He could hear everyone breathing and sniffling as they watched Dell sit up and stare back at them from only a few feet away.

"On three," said Dell. He held up his middle three fingers.

He dropped his ring finger.

Then he dropped his middle finger.

With his trigger finger up, Dell closed his eyes and took several controlled breaths. A mosquito landed on his wet arm. A pair of plump flies swarmed his head.

Dell kept his eyes closed, but smiled and dropped the last finger.

Shots rang out, but Joe couldn't watch. He looked to Dell's right. After the last shot, Joe walked over and looked down at Dell. Two bloody holes in his chest and one a few inches above his eyes. "Fucking shit."

Joe walked back to Tim's garage and sat. Tim joined, and put his arm around Joe, saying, "Me and Christian are gonna take him by for Ashley. We'll bury him tonight in the woods behind my house. First James, now Dell. We can handle it if you need to take the night."

Joe pinched the bridge of his nose. "Wonder who had the real rounds?"

"Sheeit," said Tim. "We all did, man. We all did. Dell knew it was the only way."

Joe shook his head and felt tears run down his face. He punched himself hard in the chest, but the sharp pain was ineffective. His body needed to cry.

12

TWELVE

June 18

The plan sounded simple: Four LMTVs would cordon off the main road, preventing anyone or anything from attacking the rear. The MRAP and rubber tire loader would lure the zombies to the main road, where Tim would mow them down.

Pat boarded Dell's boat, which Jeff was now running and acting as commodore for the operation. Pat's job was to oversee the setup of the gunboats and extraction boats, to direct fire toward any Zs Tim missed, and to prevent anybody from getting overly excited on the gunboats and shooting the MRAP, LMTVs, or Joe's and Tim's loaders.

Route 10 was fairly clear during the ride to the Coast Guard Yard. Pat had sent out two crews to clear the exit to 695 and the road leading there. Joe watched the abandoned cars and scattered bodies flashing by. Things were far worse up here than the previous part of the highway. Under his breath Joe grumbled about the longer route. There was a faster way, but due to the draw bridges along that road being left up, the convoy was forced to take Route 10 to the highway and double back. As they passed by the bay, they saw their small group of deadrises parked off the shore, waiting for word to move.

At the top of the road, they offloaded Tim's track loader as the LMTVs took their positions. Tim led the way, followed by Joe in the rubber tire loader and Spencer driving the MRAP.

They were rolling down Concrete Road past a large parking lot when they heard the first rounds fired by the gunboats.

Joe radioed Jeff, "You boys got eyes on the threat?"

Pat responded, "Aye, decent presence here by the water."

Tim hit the mic. "Pat, I'll be coming down Main Street—er—Ross Avenue. Soon."

Joe turned off on Bungalow Road and called Spencer. "Keep some space between us and call out if you see something. Big or small."

Joe spotted a pack of twenty Zs that had staggered from behind a big utility building as Spencer's voice came through Joe's speaker. Joe could hear the tension in his voice. "A lot of—" The radio cut out. "—softball field."

Joe's eyes widened as he saw a couple hundred Zs racing out of the softball field. "Spence, blow past me and beeline for the waterfront. We can't risk the MRAP."

Spencer came over the radio. "Oh, okay, I'm rolling."

Spencer sped past Joe and disappeared around the bend. Joe slowed his roll, hoping to keep the bulk of Zs on him. He reached in his pocket and pulled out a cigarette and lit it. "Tim, Spencer's coming in quick. Be ready. I'm not far behind." Joe blew smoke out of the corner of his mouth and immediately took another drag. He turned the corner to glimpse Spencer running over a few Zs before Spencer turned out of sight. Joe blew the horn a few times as he puffed the cigarette. "Dinner time, assholes. Come get it." Joe raised the bucket and braked to almost a stop. The Zs piled up around the loader, then Joe slammed the bucket down crushing close to a dozen of them and knocking back just as many. Joe pushed the throttle and started grinding the bucket along the road as he doubled back to the softball fields.

When Joe heard more gunfire erupt down by the water, he hoped that was Spencer getting to safety along the waterfront. As Joe arrived at the softball field he saw that the group had grown to a over a few hundred. Joe flicked his cigarette butt out the window and lit another cigarette. He turned the loader hard, causing it to tip a little. He cut the wheel back and released the throttle as he felt it correct and slam back down. Joe's heart pounded as he felt the impact on the rear of the loader and heard the banging and stomping all over the back of the cab.

Peering out the partially closed steel viewport in the back of the loader, Joe saw the weld on the air intake cracking and bending from the zombies pulling on it as they covered the back. Joe shook some off by jerking the steering back and forth as he hurled the loader forward by stomping the throttle.

The Zs continued their onslaught, crawling all over the cab as Joe turned down Ross Avenue heading for the waterfront where Pat and the team waited. Joe slowed again and tried shaking a few more off. Joe's eyes widened as the modified air intake tore off with a zombie's arm wrapped around it. Joe floored it, knowing that if anything blocked the intake, he could stall. Lights out. Night, night.

Joe continued to the end of the field. Once there, he turned around and rammed the loader into the pack that was still chasing him. The initial impact with the bucket parted the crowd, but caused the loader to slow momentarily. Joe pressed hard on the pedal and the ash from his cigarette fell across his chest and into his lap. He grabbed the radio and called out, "Team, cleaning up this pocket and then I'll head to you. Let me get a status check."

Spencer's voice came over the radio with a lot of static and echoes of gunfire. "So far, so good. I'm down here by the water."

Pat's response came as Joe neared the far edge of the field. "Tim and Spencer are down here. We're working on cleaning up the mess. More inbound. Head this way to clear up the remainder together. Over."

Tim's voice sounded excited when he responded. "Shit's all good. Hurry the fuck up so we can get this wrapped up."

Joe let out a slow breath and plowed into the pack again as he said to himself, "On the way."

As Joe neared to where the road opened up he hit the gas and slammed into the remaining pack. From a rough estimate he figured it to be about forty Zs left. The bucket was raised slightly to hit them at the midsection when he broke their ranks. As the bucket made contact, Joe slammed it into the ground, crushing the Zs who had been caught in the front. The shrieks and sound of bodies breaking was enough to send a chill up Joe's spine, but he pressed the pedal harder making sure to break their ranks before he set out to meet up with the rest of his team. Joe ripped through the crowd of Zs and looked out to see if anymore were coming. Unfortunately, there was one more group and Joe was their target.

Joe called out to Tim, "Tim, got one more pack. Gonna take them out and meet at the dock. Over."

Pat responded, but Joe had trouble hearing through the sound of the gunfire on Dell's boat. "Aye, need you."

Joe called back, "Pat, say again, you broke up."

Tim called out, "We need you to double time it. We got a lot of shitbirds piling up."

Joe laid on the pedal once more and turned into the pack. This time the pack was spread out and racing across the ball field. Joe aimed for the center of the group and hammered into them like a fullback coming through the slot. As he plowed through the Zs he realized the folly in his tactic. They had him surrounded. He was still moving but some of the Zs had made it onto the cab. Joe felt thumping on the roof of the loader. He eased off the throttle and shook it again. The Z fell from the roof and landed across the pipe. As Joe looked out the viewport on the back of the loader, the Z saw Joe and shrieked. It reached for Joe but couldn't move with the pipe piercing its stomach and protruding out its back.

Joe knew he only had a few seconds before the loader would stall, so he punched it and radioed: "Tim, need help. About to lose power and need a push into the gun boats' range."

A bunch of static crossed the radio, but no response.

Joe called Tim again, "Tim, she's boggin' down. Gonna need help. Now!"

"On my way!"

Joe straightened the loader out and floored it as he felt the power bog down again. With the sounds of snarls and banging from the Zs as they engulfed his loader, Joe pulled his pistol and radioed, "Tim, power's down, they are piled on me. I'm buried."

Joe heard the faint sound of the track loader as Tim responded, "Rolling, brother, be there soon. Lock it down and hang tight."

Joe raised his pistol at the Z trying to push into the viewport. Joe fired ten rounds into it as he pushed on the viewport to shut it, but it was stuck. Joe leaned into the side of the cab and jammed his foot into the knob they had welded onto the ports to open and close them. He pressed with all his strength, slamming it shut partially, but a hand from the dead Z hung in the port. Joe lifted his leg a few inches and kicked hard, causing the welded bolt they had used for a knob to break off. "Fuck!" Joe shouted as he pulled his Kabar and rammed it in the gap, wedging it behind the port into the steel frame.

As Joe checked the doors and ports he heard the rumble of the tracks in the distance. Joe reloaded his pistol and lit another cigarette. He had done all he could do until help arrived.

The sound of the tracks got louder and a voice came over the radio. It was Tim. "Behind ya," he said. "Brace for impact."

Joe sat in the seat and choked the wheel. His body flung forward when the blow hit. The track loader had knocked some of the Zs off, but Joe's vehicle was still covered. Tim continued pushing him.

Joe radioed, "Pat, can you see me yet? I'm flying blind here."

Pat responded for Tim to get out of there and for Joe to take cover. Surgical teams were on it.

Joe pushed forward on the bucket control, allowing the hydraulics to ease the loader bucket down before he climbed under the steering column. As he covered his ears the loader started pinging loudly from the small arms fire hitting the zombies that had climbed onto his machine.

After a minute, he heard the call. "Loaders clear. Tim and Spence make a few laps to clear the stragglers. Once we're good, Joe, we'll clear the port and get you running." Joe pulled the Kabar from the port and slid it open. He shoved the dead arm out. The softness of its skin made Joe tremble in disgust.

After a few hours of rolling around, they had killed the mass of the threat and Joe got out and cleared the intake and got the loader running.

Once the base was cleared, Pat and the boat crews pulled up to the docks and tied off. Joe, Tim, and Spencer backed down the pier.

Joe hopped out and stretched his legs. "Good work, guys. Now we find the living." He looked down the road and said, "Let's keep everyone here and we'll go building to building. Take a small team, so as not to escalate things if we find anyone."

Pat said, "Sure. We'll take the MRAP. In case we need to fall back."

"Spence," said Joe, "you'll be in the MRAP. Keep us in sight. The rest of my team is on me. We will go building to building. Check your weapons and grab more ammo. Roll out in five."

As the team broke up to reload and get ready, Joe told Pat, "You stay here with the boats and equipment. If we call, come running."

"Aye aye. We'll standby for egress or support."

Joe racked a round into his rifle and let it fall back over to his side as he pulled his pistol and made sure it was loaded. "Any luck we won't need you, but we'll let ya know if we find anyone."

Pat's eyes stayed fixed on Joe, acknowledging him with a single nod. He walked away without a word as Joe turned and headed for his team.

Spencer kept the MRAP a short distance behind, which allowed him to keep an eye on the team's six as they entered. The first few buildings yielded no survivors. Most of the outer buildings along the first road had supplies but appeared to have been empty for a while.

Joe turned the team up toward the barracks where he saw a window open.

As they searched a barracks along the edge of the base, a couple ran past them as they were clearing the third floor. The team raced down the stairs to find the couple facing Spencer with their hands in the air.

"Easy now," said Joe. "We're here to help."

The frail brunette girl appeared to be in her early 20s. She looked terrified. "Last guy with a gun who told me that sodomized my mother and slit her throat when he was finished."

"There aren't words to describe how terrible that is. I'm sorry you had to witness that, and that your mother had to endure it. That's not us, I promise, for what it's worth." Joe stuck his hand out for a shake, saying, "And if we found someone like that, we'd put a bullet in their head immediately, if not sooner."

The girl recoiled from Joe's hand, her right shoulder now pushing against the wall. The guy she was with had a slightly bigger profile, although still skinny for his bone structure. He swung his head to flick his hair out of his face and shook Joe's hand. "Name's Chuck. This is my sister, Jade."

"You alone?" asked Joe.

"Nobody else here," said Chuck. "We were the outpost watch. Let's go back up and we can call in for you. Fair warning, the captain doesn't like strangers on his base."

Joe went to the MRAP and radioed Pat. "Pat, found survivors. Sending Spence to get you." As Joe let go of the mic and looked at Spencer, he said, "Double time, bro."

When Spencer returned with Pat, they followed Chuck into the building. Once they reached the third floor, Joe led the way into the room. Inside, Pat found the radio sitting next to an old M16 and a case of ammo. Across the room were boxes of MREs and a small duffel bag of clothes.

Pat handed the radio to Chuck, who turned it to channel eight and said, "Base, Outpost. Need to speak to CO, over."

A few seconds ticked by before a raspy voice replied, "Outpost, Base. This is the CO. Report, over."

Chuck handed the radio to Pat. "Base, Outpost. You are speaking with Lieutenant Commander Patrick Miller of the United States Navy. I am calling to inform you that I request your audience for a meeting at the main piers in twenty minutes. We have cleared your base as well as we could in the few hours we had. If you fear attack, give us your location and we can pick you up. Over."

The radio went silent for a minute. "Outpost, Base. You are clearly a moron or a fool. In either case, you are trespassing on government property. Meeting at pier confirmed, where you can explain your actions. Be there in *fifteen*. Over."

Pat gave the radio back to Chuck. "He was pleasant."

"He's always been wound tight. And having decaying flesh milling about hasn't helped his demeanor any."

Joe raised an eyebrow at Pat. "Better hope your government friends can air-drop some asshole repellent. Stat."

As they pulled up to the pier, Joe saw five heavily-armed men and an older gray-haired man in his full dress-whites. Judging by the scowl on the CO's face, Joe doubted he'd comply with their demands. "You seeing this?"

Pat said, "I'll handle it. He'll come to understand one way or another."

Spencer manned the MRAP, while everyone climbed out of the back.

The CO led his security detail toward them.

Pat took the front, raised and was met with a salute. Sean, Tim, and Joe caught themselves saluting as well.

The CO lowered his salute, greeted Pat, then glared at Joe's team. He introduced himself as Captain Bradley Trudoe. Joe was surprised that rather than thank them, he posed the question as to why he shouldn't have them all shot for trespassing.

Pat extended his hand, saying, "Lieutenant Commander Patrick Miller. These are a few of my guys who have been clearing Maryland of its cancer. I have orders to use your base for the purpose of staging our continued push into Baltimore City."

"That sounds swell, *Patty*. But I, too, have orders. Namely, defending this base by all means necessary, including, but not limited to, executing trespassers with grandiose notions of how they're going to save the world."

"Sir, these orders come from the Secretary of Defense. I didn't mean any disrespect. I only assumed you wanted the shortest, simplest answer."

Trudoe's face shone bright red. After a moment his breathing slowed, his jaws still flexed as he ground his teeth looking over the people in Pat's group. "Is that so? I should what, take you at your word? Tell me, *Lieutenant*, some guy comes and tells you that the Secretary of—oh, it doesn't matter, let's go with the Secretary of State—that the Secretary of State wants you to relinquish all your weapons and let this stranger, who randomly shows up to your house, by the way, to let him shove those weapons straight up your ass. Are you going to let him do it because *he* says the Secretary of State says so?"

Pat remained composed, even as the captain's security detail started to get a bit too antsy, moving their rifles about. Pat motioned for "weapons down" as he slowly reached into his breast pocket and pulled out the sat phone. "Captain, I will put you in touch with chain of command."

Pat dialed and waited before saying, "Admiral, this is Miller. I need you to relay our orders to base CO." There was a long pause. "Full bird, sir. No, he hasn't." Pat smiled, "No, sir, but he did kindly remind us that we were trespassing on his base. Thank you, sir. Aye, sir, will do." Handing the phone to Captain Trudoe, Patrick said, "It's SecDef, McLaven."

Captain Trudoe squinted and slowly took the phone from Pat. "This is Captain Bradley Trudoe, who exactly am I speaking with?" A pause. "*Bull*shit. Don't buy it for a minute. We haven't been contacted in months. You would know the channels. You may be able to bullshit the National Guard, but—excuse me?"

The captain was pacing. His face was flush, but it no longer appeared angry, only confused. As he paced back and forth, his security detail's posture softened. Joe realized that, with the exception of the captain, everyone was hoping this was going to go easy. The captain stopped pacing, focused on the ground. Something happened, because he now looked angry. Joe leaned back and whispered to Tim, "Something's wrong." Tim nodded, never taking his finger off the trigger or his eyes off the captain.

After another long pause, the captain ended the call with, "Okay. Standing by." He shoved the phone into Pat's chest. "He has one minute to validate his claim and then I will remove you from this base, by your own accord or mine. I haven't decided."

Captain Trudoe tapped his watch twice. "Men, on my mark, these vagrants have forty-five seconds to vacate the premises or use force to eliminate them." Staring at his watch, Bradley counted. "Thirty-eight. Thirty-seven. Thirty-six. Thirty-five. ..."

Joe readied himself to reach for his pistol, his hand gravitating toward it slowly.

Pat told the captain to stand down. "The call is coming."

The captain didn't flinch. "Twenty-five. Twenty-four. Twenty-three. ..."

Joe looked at Tim and his guys, then back to Pat, his heart racing. "He gets to five, we draw back to the MRAP. I refuse to have survived all this shit only to get shot by this asshole."

"Sixteen. Fifteen. Fourteen. ..."

Pat reached for his sidearm and undid the clip. He eyed the captain's security detail, saying, "I am warning you all, do not fire. Any overreaction on your part and we'll be forced to protect ourselves and our mission."

"Nine. Eight. Seven. ..."

Joe clicked the safety off his rifle and swung it up in position. One of the captain's men positioned himself in front of the captain while the others fanned out. Joe's guys spread out in response. As Joe drew a bead on the security detail, Pat shouted, "No! Stand down, all of you. He will call."

Joe spit at the ground. "Fuck that. Tell them to stand down before we put them down! My team, if they fire, kill them all!"

Captain Trudoe put his hand up. "Three. Two. ..." Then the radio transmission came: "Captain, codeword Raven, codeword Raven. I repeat, codeword Raven."

The captain's face turned white. "Stand down, stand down!"

After a minute, the captain said, "Commander, call the Admiral."

Pat pulled the phone and called.

"Sir, thank you. No, everyone is okay. Mmhmm. Mmhmm. Aye, sir." Pat said, "Captain, phone's for you."

Captain Trudoe took the phone and walked away. Joe could hear screaming coming through the receiver, turning the captain's walk into a stride. After a few minutes, the captain returned. Still on the phone, he proclaimed, "Understood. Sir, you have to understand—we will take care of it. Yes, sir. Full access at his disposal."

Pat smiled and nodded his head as the captain finished talking. "I can do that," said Trudoe. "I would only ask that, as your guys quote, 'liberate goods,' you make sure to restock us. That said, we also have one mission that should be top of the list, and that's clearing Curtis Bay. There are a group of convicts who escaped from the prison who are hostile and need to be dealt with. Yes, Admiral, I understand." He hung up and returned the phone to Pat.

Tim broke the silence. "Got some shitbirds, sir?"

"Something like that."

* * *

As the workboat rounded the point, Joe removed his earpiece. "Peaceful out here. Way more than it's going to be tomorrow." The chemical company where he and Sean used to work came into view. "Sean, you looking forward to going back to work tomorrow?"

Sean gave the old plant the finger and spit in the water. "Wonder if anyone we work with is holed up there?"

Joe stared at the department along the waterfront. The siding had been blown off in a few spots on the fifth floor. Rusty chemical tanks sat in their usual spots out in the tank farm.

For as much as he had disliked this place in the past, he longed for it now. Mediocre coffee. Lunchroom refrigerators that reeked of expired food. Men talking shit to each other. Men talking lots of shit to their supervisors. Joe missed hitting the turnstile outside the gate before each shift. He missed how, in order to help get through the last workday before a day off, the men always said the same thing when passing by each other. They'd say, "Last one. *Laaaast* one."

What Joe missed was the predictability of it all. Predictable is comfortable.

Joe told Sean, "This time tomorrow we should know. We've had to help a few old friends sleep already."

"I'd sleep everyone last one of them like that," he said with the snap of his fingers, "if it'd bring back my dad or Jenna."

"I hear you, brother. I hear you." Joe said, "But hey, listen. We can't cowboy this shit tomorrow. One misplaced shot and we hit the wrong tank, we're toast."

Sean lifted his binoculars and scanned the waterfront. "Put that in the safety briefing tomorrow morning." He dragged a hand in the air across his face, saying, "Dumbfucks beware." Sean searched the shorelines and said, "There has to be a better spot to hit than work. Maybe the shipyard. Or better yet the strip club. Gotta be something more worthwhile over there." Sean checked the opposing shoreline.

Joe rolled his eyes. "Come on, man, be serious. There's a lot of shit that could be useful at work. Besides, who knows: What if some of our friends are there?"

Sean let out a half groan, half laugh, and kept scanning across the water. As Joe waited for a response, Sean's arms tensed up and his knuckles grew white around the binoculars. "Whoa, whoa, whoa. Stop the boat."

Jeff dropped the old diesel out of gear and backed down for a second to steady the boat.

Sean leaned forward. "Damn if it ain't. Over there, take a look."

Joe peered through his rifle scope. A group of people stood in the parking lot of Fantasies Nightclub. In the bed of a white Chevy 1500 pickup sat a broad-chested man on a turquoise beach chair. The man had long hair and held a chrome revolver. He was pointing it at a group of women and children and appeared to be yelling.

Joe lowered the rifle, shaking his head. Three loud cracks rang out and Joe flinched.

13

THIRTEEN

June 19

The entrance to the plant was barricaded by concrete Jersey walls.

Joe stopped about ten car lengths out and lit a cigarette. He took a drag, blew it out the window, then stomped the gas. He plowed through the concrete barriers and said, "I hope they listened."

If they punctured an anhydrous ammonia tank or knocked out a nitric acid pipe and got sprayed, you're talking loss of eyesight and skin. Caustic. Phosphoric acid. Hydrochloric acid. Titanium tetrachloride. Maimed, melted, burned, or worse—dead, dead, dead.

Once inside the chemical plant's yard, Joe radioed Spencer and Tim, "Okay, guys. So, Tim, you'll follow me around to the waterfront. Spencer, go down to the left and loop back to the waterfront by the piers. Remember: one screw-up here and we're all goners."

Tim had music coming through his mic as he called in, an old Rob Zombie song called Thunderkiss 65. Joe smiled as he heard the song just before Tim yelled into the mic, "Oh, boy. Got company, four o'clock. About thirty coming in hot."

After a few more passes and a lot of scraping to push the bodies down the hill into the water, the chemical yard was fairly clean. Some stragglers remained, but most of them were now being eaten by the vultures and seagulls in Curtis Bay.

Joe grabbed the keys, his pack and his rifle, and climbed out of the loader. The team assembled on the pier.

"All right, guys," said Joe. "We're going to each department together. I got point with Sean taking the rear. If we get separated, follow one of us or Spencer." Joe said to Christian, "I want you to stay here with the equipment in case anyone comes down here."

The G-11 warehouse was the first stop. When they walked in Tim looked at the standing water that surrounded hundreds of metal drums. "That shit just water?"

Sean tapped his boot in it, making small splashes. "Just water. Without power, the pumps can't drain it."

The place was old and dark. It had a rotting catwalk system above that overlooked the sprawling space. Tall and wide stacks of drums piled all over caused odd shadows to be cast about.

Joe asked Tim to take position on a double stack of drums. Nothing in the room was volatile, so firing ammunition wasn't an issue.

Tim was ready with his M4 pointed across the warehouse.

Joe grabbed a chunk of concrete and hurled it toward the center of the warehouse. It hit the top of a drum and bounced off, banging into multiple drums before splashing down into the water.

Tim hollered out, "Two bogeys, ten o'clock."

Joe set his rifle across a couple drums in front of him and took aim. "Three! Two! One!"

Two shots zipped across the building, splattering blood, brain, and bone on the back wall.

With his rifle leading the charge, Joe ran up for a closer look. When he reached the bodies, he stared and blinked repeatedly as sweat dripped down and burned his eyes. He lowered his rifle and sighed.

Spencer and Sean came over.

"Damn," said Sean. "That's Skip and Terry, ain't it?"

A loud crash came from behind them.

"Five more, one o'clock, coming in fast," said Tim. "Get the fuck out of the way!"

Joe, Sean, and Spencer fired into the small group of Zs. Spencer hit the first one as it weaved around a pallet holding three drums, the bullet tunneling through its chest and lodging into another Z's sternum.

Two Zs remained upright, staggering forward until three others came from behind and plowed over them as they charged for Joe, Sean, and Spencer.

Spencer fired at the leading Z, but his gun jammed. He shouted expletives and pulled the handle to eject the round while Joe and Sean moved around him and shot at the Z until it relented and fell, its head whacking the rim of a metal drum on its way to the ground. Sean's magazine was empty, and Joe fired his last round and hit the far wall as the other two closed in.

With two Zs nearly at arm's length and Joe out of bullets, he let the sling take his rifle as he dropped to one knee, pulled his pistol, and unloaded ten rounds into the one closest to him. It fell face first to the ground, its forehead landing on top of Joe's front boot. Spencer unjammed his gun, but had no time to aim, so he lunged and hit the oncoming Z with the butt of his rifle, stunning it and giving Sean enough time to finish his reload and fire a few rounds to kill the last Z.

"Dickheads." Joe kicked the one closest to him in its ribs, then moved around the room and back to where Skip and Terry were laying. As he turned the corner he saw Sean taking something out of their wallets. When Joe splashed in a puddle Sean quickly jammed something into his pocket and swung the wallets toward Joe, saying, "Yeah, it was them. Figured I'd make sure."

* * *

The building clearance was going well. Four down, five to go, and a few small outbuildings along the perimeter. The group had noted that they only found zombies where there was a lot of standing water, so they were hoping the next building would be dry and clear.

The next building had Joe nervous because it was a "No Fire" building. The center building was called the Flammables Storage House, an old four-story warehouse. Though structurally sound, it always looked like a hard wind

120

could knock it down. The siding kept the rain out but was missing in so many places now that it created weird shadows and reflections off the puddles on the floor. It housed tanks full of ethanol and kerosene.

Joe said, "This place is fucked up. A couple small control rooms up top for the bridge crane and another control room where they'd pump materials around the yard. Problem is, we can't shoot and there are a lot of blind corners."

Spencer let his rifle fall to his side and picked up a stainless steel pipe from the ground by the wall. Everyone else moved around the vicinity searching for trash that could double as a weapon, with the exception of Tim, who pulled a large blade from his hip. Tim smiled as he used the blade to shave his forearm. Joe shook his head and turned back to the group. "I need at least one guy. Any volunteers?"

Spencer chewed the skin on the inside of his bottom lip. Sean shrugged and stepped forward, but Tim said, "Sheeit, I'm game."

"All right," said Joe. "Knives only, no guns. Sean and Spencer, you guys set a perimeter. But remember, no shooting toward this building."

"Ain't my first rodeo, man," said Sean. "Relax. Used to work here, too, remember?"

Joe looked at Sean for several moments before he pulled the Kabar from the sheath and walked into the building.

Tim whispered, "Quiet in here. Lucky for you, Joe, I've got hands that could choke a bear, if it came to it."

Joe led the way, a relatively straight path to the stairs for the control room. The path was crowded by large tanks on one side and double-stacked plastic drums on the other.

Something moved in the shadows. Joe patted the air, signaling for Tim to get low and stay quiet. As Joe crept toward the shadows, he crossed a small figure crouched down and using its hands to cup pooled rain water from the floor to its mouth. It was a small woman. Rather, it used to be a woman. Joe hesitated. He reminded himself it wasn't human, that it wasn't alive. It wasn't female in the truest sense of the word. It was death and it was insatiable.

Joe advanced ten paces when the woman stood and turned. It growled, squared up with Joe, and charged forward, its arms extended and hands open. As it closed the distance between them, Joe kicked it in the stomach, where it stumbled backward, buckled over and coughed blood on the floor. Joe reached and grabbed its left wrist, and it came forward again, but he jerked the arm past and plunged his knife into its throat. The Z dropped.

Joe turned around, glanced at Tim who was standing a few feet behind. "She was not an employee here." Joe bent over, pulled the knife out of its throat. He shook blood off his knife and said, "Least not from my memory."

"Seems weird, don't you think? How we don't see many women and children with this—disease?" Tim reached into his pocket and pulled a pouch of Beechnut tobacco out and grabbed a wad. "Want some?"

Joe declined with a short wave. "From what Alex has told me, it has a much higher kill rate on the elderly and kids. Like the flu. And the women, Alex was saying the Alphas kill them first when they get hungry."

Tim nodded. "You figure they probably move slower. Less muscle. So they starve to—shit, what do you call dead who die?"

"*Less muscle?* That's some sexist shit right there, you know that?" Joe winked at Tim.

Tim smiled and shrugged. "I'm a pig."

After they moved onward about fifty feet, Joe saw footprints and blood in the dust at the top of the stairs. Joe pointed to it then held his finger to his lips.

They approached the door. Through the small window pane they watched a wrinkled, gray-haired zombie walk across the room. Tim said, "My turn." As he reached for the doorknob, Joe grabbed his arm. "Wait."

The Z stood at the sink and cupped water from inside the sink into its hands. After a few sips, it walked over to the window and swung its hands wildly at a pigeon stooped on a railing just outside.

"That's Will Lemons. Used to work with that guy."

"Was he a friend?" Tim asked.

"He wasn't really what you would call a friend, but I didn't hate the guy. He was bitter, often angry, often drunk. But he could be funny. And he was smart." Joe reached into his pocket and pulled out a cigarette which he stuck behind his ear. "I should do it. Watch my back."

"How about we go together?"

Joe nodded slightly. "All right."

Tim opened the door and Joe walked in slowly. The Z stood about ten feet away moaning and staring at the bird outside the window. Joe stepped on a candy wrapper and the Z turned and charged Joe. Tim darted across the room for something and the Z crashed into Joe, slamming him into the wall. It opened its mouth wide and lunged its head at Joe and bit down just as Joe got the palm of his hand under its chin. It growled and barred its brown teeth centimeters away from Joe's nose when Tim brought a rusted pipe down on the back of its head. The Z fell to the side and Tim hit him twice more in the temple region until it split open and blood trickled out.

With his eyes on the dead Z, Tim asked Joe if he was okay.

Joe said no, as a matter of fact he wasn't. But it wasn't the time for a therapy session.

Joe tossed the cigarette from behind his ear by the Z's side and said, "Last one, brother. Last one."

Clearing the buildings had taken four hours before they reached the two-story admin building nestled in the center of the yard. Joe had been hopeful that there would be people inside, but after a thorough search all they found were dead bodies with bite marks and missing flesh.

With a few hours of daylight left, the team salvaged a few heavy trucks from the main warehouse. They grabbed a couple large fuel tanks full of diesel and regular gasoline, as well as a couple pallets of Gatorade that the chemical company had once kept in stock for employees. In the maintenance building, Tim started making plans for fabricating equipment and rigging up vehicles with heavy plates.

"Good, but it's getting late," Joe said. "We gotta stop by the Coast Guard Yard before we call it a day."

When they arrived at the Coast Guard Yard, Pat was waiting with Alex.

Joe asked Alex, "Where's Cara?"

Alex bit his lip. "She's home now."

"What'ya mean *now*?"

Alex's hand moved like he was about to conduct a symphony. "Let's talk about it on the ride home."

Joe's nostrils flared, but before he could respond Pat cut the conversation off. "I've already talked to Jimmy, Sarge, Matt, and Jeff, so I'm gonna make this simple. We are going to make contact with the gang in Curtis Bay tomorrow morning. Your job is to provide overwatch in case things go sideways."

Joe's chin pulsed as he clenched down on his teeth. "You didn't think to talk to us about this first?"

"This makes more sense. You are better equipped for taking the perimeter on this one. If things go wrong it will be invaluable to know how these guys move."

"So, what the fuck? Jimmy and his boys are bait?"

Alex grabbed Joe's arm. "No, nothing like that. We just want the best we have watching their backs. We figure they won't attack us on first contact. If that was their goal they would have already tried to. Trust me, I don't like the idea either, but it makes the most sense."

Joe looked over at Ryan and Tim, saying, "We need to go put together a plan. Everyone meet at my house after dinner. Meeting is over. Alex you're riding with me. Spencer you go with Sean."

Pat went to say something and Joe put up his hand. "You've said enough. We'll take it from here."

As they drove down the highway Joe pulled a pack of cigarettes from the center console and beat them on his thigh. After opening them and lighting one he said to Alex, "Cara. What about her?"

Alex squirmed in his seat. "She left this morning while I was dealing with one of the other teams and went on a run."

Joe's face went red. "She did what? How the fuck did she manage that?"

Alex stuttered for a second before he formed a coherent sentence. "She has been helpful and usually on point. But lately, she has been hanging around an older Vietnam vet that she said you knew. Jim, Jim Shaw I think."

Joe's face lost all expression. "Jim Shaw? He was like a father to me. Taught me a ton of stuff after mine died. You remember him. Lived a few houses up. What does he have to do with Cara making a run?"

"He has been training with Cara and a few others that were preparing for runs. I didn't think it mattered. She actually is a really good shot and her doing so well motivated others to step up and take on more."

"What kind of training?" asked Joe.

"They work on some hand to hand stuff, small arms, and rifle. Cara was even showing them how to throw knives."

"How did she manage to worm her way into a run?"

"From what I gathered, she convinced Jim. She only took watch outside of the houses, but she did take out five Zs that came when they were inside clearing. Jim said she performed well, while the other guy who was posted up with her hesitated."

Joe could feel his pulse beating out of his neck. "Why did Jim let her go? There has to be more than that."

Alex stared out the window. "I thought the same thing. But I think you already know how she convinced him."

Joe flicked the cigarette out the window.

"She wanted to be able to hold her own."

Joe grabbed the top of his head and ran his fingers through his hair. "I don't—I don't know what to do here. Can you promise me to keep her occupied 'til things get done?"

Alex nodded quickly. "Yeah, I will keep her close or I will make sure she stays home."

Joe stared out at the highway. "I appreciate it. Just keep her busy so I can focus on this fucking mess Pat is getting us into."

"There is something else, but it may be nothing."

Joe rolled his eyes. "Just get it out."

"It's Sean. He, well—he has been leaving at night, but no one knows where he's been going. The other night he left with his rifle and that pack he always carries. The checkpoints say that he drives off and they see him a few hours later. I don't know if you want to ask him, but I figured you should know."

Joe's hands ground into the worn out leather on the steering wheel. "I will talk to him. I heard him leave a few times but didn't bother to ask. Honestly, as long as he has his head together and is there on time it isn't my problem."

Alex's bottom lip began to draw down a little. "I think it is your problem. He is staying at the house with our families. If he is a liability—"

Joe punched the steering wheel. "No, he isn't a liability. He has just been through some shit. If he starts showing up smelling like a brewery, then I will worry. You know how shit was for me when Dad died. He'll come out of this fine. If he wants to go ride off at night for a while then who am I to question it?"

14

FOURTEEN

June 20

Tensions ran high as the fog lifted from the brackish waters of Curtis Bay. The poor visibility had delayed Jimmy's team's deployment by more than an hour.

Joe paced back and forth on the bridge, listening to Jimmy's open mic. "Ryan, you see anything?"

Ryan looked up from the scope of the M4. "Nothing. Nobody posted anywhere. These fuckers can't be that stupid."

"Spencer, you? See anything?"

"Couple guys by the fueling dock. They didn't seem to mind when Jimmy's boat pulled up."

Joe grimaced. "Maybe we have these guys wrong. Maybe they killed that guy because he raped someone or killed somebody."

"What's your gut tell you?" Ryan said.

Joe paused. "That these guys are fucked up."

Minutes passed and Tim radioed in. "Six guys armed, heading to the pier."

Joe scanned the area. A window on a house barge slid open. Joe radioed, "Be advised, shooter located on house barge. Tim, see if you can get a better angle on him."

A bearded man propped the front of his rifle out the window, just enough to use the sill as a rest for the barrel. Tim watched as the man stuffed a pinch of tobacco behind his bottom lip then took sight behind the scope. Tim called out on the radio, "Copy, I have him in my view. He's targeting Jimmy's crew. Request to engage."

Joe had the mic to his mouth, about to respond, when Jimmy said to wait until they meet with the six guys heading to the boat. But if things go south, take him out fast.

Sean piped up. "Sniper spotted, top of green fuel tank. Permission to engage?"

Jimmy said, "Negative. Tim and Sean, maintain visual only. Do not engage."

Joe's jaw was clenched. Ryan smiled at him, saying, "Don't like his call?"

"Do Iraqis shit in the sand?" Joe radioed, "Tim, Sean, if shit jumps off, you know what to do."

Jimmy radioed, "They're coming. I assume the leader is the one in the center. Short gray hair, receding hairline. Has an eagle on his neck. Could be the German coat of arms, can't be sure. Actually, I'm seeing lots of poorly done prison tats, but none that scream gang affiliation. All are armed. The three guys behind him carrying rifles look like his enforcers. More shitty tattoos, but nothing out of the ordinary. The two up front keep scratching their necks and arms. Junkies, by the looks of it."

Joe noticed that the long-haired man he saw on the truck from the previous day wasn't with them and that Jimmy had turned off the hot mic on his radio. They were going to have to go off of sight alone.

Through his scope Joe watched as Jimmy nodded, then raised an arm and waved at the approaching group. The man in front returned the gesture as he walked down the dock of the shipyard. When he was a few feet away from the stern of the boat, he said something to Jimmy.

Jimmy responded and finished his sentence with a smile.

Neck Tattoo picked at a scab on his shoulder but said nothing.

Jimmy responded and the guy straightened his posture, brought his chin down.

Jimmy had the radio in his hand by his side and used his thumb to squeeze the side key. "You guys all from around here?"

With a raspy voice, Neck Tattoo said, "You could say that. But enough with the bullshit, you want passage through our city, you pay the toll."

Jimmy kept his eyes on the man with the neck tattoo, but the man was somewhere else, staring off in the distance. Joe swung his focus from the tattered old dock, saw a flock of seagulls that Neck Tattoo was looking at. They were diving in and picking at something in the water. Joe swung back to focus on Jimmy and heard the raspy voice continue. "Let's start with those guns, then we'll consider your request."

Jimmy said, "That's off the table."

The man stuck a blue toothpick in his mouth and moved it around with his tongue. "Nothing's off the table."

Jimmy laughed. "Look, pal—"

"Ain't your pal, chief."

"All right, well, you made it clear you've got no interest in helping us. But I'm telling you, it's in your best interest, if you catch my drift."

Neck Tattoo pulled his toothpick out. "See, I was trying to be nice." He peeked over his shoulder at his men, then popped his toothpick back in and cradled it in his cheek. "I was trying to be a real sport. Civil like. And then you had to go and act tough. So, let me explain this to you differently. Give me your guns or I will take them from you. And perhaps—*perhaps* I won't piss on your dead body afterwards."

Jimmy rolled his shoulders. "Let's not go this route. I don't want to waste any bullets."

Neck Tattoo laughed. "You have no chance. I'm telling you right now—"

Jimmy's radio went out. Silence.

Jimmy brought up his rifle and fired at the man to his left. The bullet tore through his chest, dropped him to his knees. Gunfire erupted from both sides.

Joe took aim and fired at one of the enforcers nearest to him, hitting him in the stomach. Joe raised his aim, heard a loud boom and ducked in reaction. Over the radio came Sean's voice: "Sniper down."

Joe fired the next shot into his target.

Tim radioed, "Snipers hit, but not down. Sean, put one through the wall of the barge to finish him. Fucker's still moving."

Joe turned to the barge where the living quarters sat. The sniper was setting back up, even though he was bleeding from his stomach. Joe radioed, "Sean, second floor, third window from the right."

The sniper that Tim had shot got a round off before Joe heard the blast from the .50BMG. Sean's shot tore through the wall and chest of the sniper, laying him out on the floor and splattering most of him on the room's back wall.

Joe called out as the firing died down, saying, "Everyone report in."

Joe's team called out clear, but then Sarge radioed in from the boat. "Jimmy is down, multiple rounds to vest. One in the shoulder, another through his thigh. In and out. Boat is hit, taking on water, but still running. Also, two pussies dove in when everything popped off. Any takers?"

Joe scanned the area. The snipers were dead along with four of the six who had shown up for the meet. Jimmy was alive, although leaking blood all over the deck. Sarge began trying to stabilize him with the med bag. Meanwhile, Jeff pointed a snubnosed revolver at the two men in the water. He shouted commands laced with profanities before tossing them a ring buoy.

Matt stood at the boat's helm, ready to take off.

* * *

At the Coast Guard Yard, the men Jeff had fished out of the bay were sitting at a small table in the cafe when Joe walked in. Joe's team was seated in the corner having what appeared to be a heated discussion.

Joe stood between the two strangers and his team. Rather than get into a debate Joe headed for the table where the two sat. When he got to the edge of the table Joe stood over them with his fists pressed against the table. "What are your names?"

The first guy looked up. "Bull."

The blonde hair guy said, "I'm Joker," as he showed him the tattoo of a skull with a jester's hat on his forearm.

Joe pointed at the track marks on Joker's arms. "I'm guessing that's how you know Shane."

Joker pulled his arms in and hid them under the table. "Great work, detective. Observations like that, you must've been valedictorian."

"How did Shane become the man in charge of Curtis Bay?"

Joker turned to the side, looked down at the floor. "The dude took us in when everything went to fuck all shit. That's all I got to say there, Boss."

Joe asked Bull, "How about you? Your junkie ass have anything to add?"

Bull looked up, then back at the floor. "Nah, not shit to say."

Joe felt his rage rising as he stared at them. He walked toward his team's table and waved for Tim and Ryan to come over. Joe said, "Take them and find two rooms. I want them separated when I get back. Think there's some empty offices next door."

As Joe walked away he noticed Bull was watching him from the table. Joe smiled as he pushed the door open and headed to the infirmary.

At the infirmary, he found Doctor Jeff. Joe waited until he was done with one of the Coast Guard's guys before he went and sat on the edge of the bed. "I need something. Something a junkie would get excited over."

Jeff's face looked grim. "What for?"

"Bait."

Jeff stepped back. "You want to use the little bit of painkillers I have to bribe a junkie?"

"Jeff, I don't have time. Trust me, it's the best option. Besides, as bad as they look they are gonna get worse soon if I don't give them something small. We don't need two shit birds going into withdraws on top of everything else."

Jeff went over to a cabinet and got out a jar of pills. He dumped a few into a small baggy then put the rest away. As he walked over he tossed the Ziploc to Joe. "Hope it's worth it." Over his shoulder, Jeff said, "Make 'em last. We don't have many."

Joe stuffed the pills in his pocket and hurried to the offices. When he got there, he saw Tim first and asked him, "Which one is in there?"

"Jackass. And Bullshit's next door."

Joe looked down the hall to Ryan and nodded before ducking into Joker's room. In the room stood a metal desk, a few chairs, and some file cabinets along the wall. Joe scanned the room, walked in, and sat across from Joker.

"Okay, it's just you and me so you can drop the tough guy shit. Tell me what I wanna know and I'll make it worth your while."

Joe pulled the bag of pills out and sat one on the table.

Joker spit on the table. "Fuck you."

Joe put the pill back in the bag. "Wrong answer, bitch." Joe jumped across the table and got both hands around the back of Jokers head. Joker pulled back but Joe pulled hard and slammed his face into the desk with all his force. Joker screamed and Joe let go, sending Joker flying backwards and off the chair. "I'm gonna ask you one more time," said Joe. "Ready to talk?"

Joker's nose was bleeding down the front of his shirt. He wiped his face.

Joe took a step forward and Joker's fists balled up.

Joker lunged and tried to swing. Joe dodged the blow and kneed Joker in his midsection and followed the knee with a hard left hook, knocking Joker into the wall and onto the floor. Joe jumped on top of Joker and began hitting him, saying, "I'm gonna. Ask. You. Again. Do. You. Have. Anything. Of. Use. You. Dumb. Junkie. Fuck."

Joe stood and stepped back. As Joker tried to peel himself from the floor he spat blood across the room. "Get fucked, asshole. Snitches get stitches."

"They aren't the only ones, douchebag." Joe exited the room and closed the door. He waved Ryan over. "Could Bull hear that?"

Ryan's left lip curled up. "Half the base did, bro."

"Good, take him to Doc. I'm gonna go have a conversation with contestant number two."

Tim asked Joe, "Don't want one of us to stick around in case the other one gets squirrely?"

"He doesn't want what his buddy just got. I'll be fine."

Joe waited until Tim and Ryan had left with Joker before he entered the room Bull was in. The room was similar to the one Joker had been in except for a few motivational posters on the wall and a desk with a couple coasters and some small stationary behind a name plate that read, DAVID JENNINGS.

Bull looked terrified.

Joe pulled the bag of pills out and took a seat. "Okay, I started with your dumbass friend, but I have a good feeling you're the one who's gonna wanna work with me. I can see that you're sensible."

Bull was trembling as Joe slid one of the pills across the table. Bull took the pill and tucked it underneath a coaster. He then pushed and twisted the coaster, crushing the pill, which he cut it into a line of powder. He leaned down and snorted it up. After wiping his face he told Joe that the guy he wants, his last name was Chauncey. He was the guy who cornered and beat up several cops when they raided his house years ago. Got off on some technicality. Supposedly he killed some people, too. Never got pinned for it, though.

Joe played with the bag of pills as he stared at Bull. "Okay, so, Shane took you guys in, then what? Were you all in jail when this—how'd you put it—'fuck all shit' happened?"

Bull flipped the coaster over and wiped the residue off the coaster. He licked his finger, wiped it up, and rubbed it onto his gums. "Prison, not jail. But yeah. When things got real bad, they opened the doors and all the COs left. From there, escaping was easy and we came down here, happened to run into Shane. He said we had the choice of working for him or becoming worm food. And a few days ago he killed three people simply because they refused to work for him, so I'd say we chose right."

Joe slid another pill across the table. "Sounds like he was the dickhead we saw out front of Fantasies. How many people does he have under him now?"

"Hard to say, maybe fifty? But they are spread out. He has guns, like an artillery's worth or some shit, and some of the guys in his crew are ex-military. He lives above the bar by the little park with his girlfriends."

"That everything?"

Bull squirmed in his seat as he rolled the pill between his fingers. "I, I do know he has some guys stationed in empty houses around that park. He keeps them spread out in teams of two and four. They do them walk arounds a lot. Even at night."

Joe stared through Bull.

"That's it, man. We only ever went in that close a few times. He kept us at the edge of town by the fuel place. Said when we proved worth it, we could get in closer. One of his guys was in our group. The guy the boat guy shot.

He was in charge of us. That's all I know."

"If I'm honest, I'm not sure what to do with you." Joe cracked his knuckles. "For now, get up and let's get you some food. While we head over, think about anything that could be important you forgot to mention."

As Joe walked Bull toward the café, he saw Pat heading for him with two of the Coasties.

Pat asked, "Done with him?"

"For the time being. He did well enough to grab a bite to eat."

Pat told the two Coasties to take Bull.

As Joe told Pat what Bull had said, Pat stopped him. "That guy Chauncey is a major player in this area. We need to eliminate that threat before it becomes one to us."

Joe's face went blank. "That solves it. Time to go murder an apocalyptic drug lord? Shit, if you would've told me that I would one day utter a phrase like that." Joe laughed. "Don't get me wrong: I'm sure we can make it work. But he did just see our Sunday punch, so I'm sure he's going to make some adjustments next time."

"Most of those guys were prisoners who probably joined up after they were let out. That was his B team."

Joe grabbed the brim of his hat and adjusted it a few times. "Where's Alex?"

Pat checked his watch. "He left fifteen minutes ago. Shouldn't be much longer."

"We need something more than 'we need to go eliminate the threat.' It's one thing racing around shooting Zs. People aren't that stupid."

"Most people, yes." Pat nodded. "If you don't think your guys are up to it we can go around. But the fastest way into Baltimore is straight through and we don't have much time to cut a new path."

Joe could feel his skin crawling. "You didn't send us this way to get at this fucking dope dealer, did you?"

The corner of Pat's mouth curled in a half smile. "Sadly, no, but when we opted to go this way, it came onto my radar. This guy is only going to become worse if we open up the roads around him. Either we take him now or after he shoots another one of our guys. Speaking of, Jimmy should be okay. Going to be sore as shit for a few days, sure, but he should be able to run the boat again soon."

Joe closed his eyes and exhaled. "You really gonna use Jimmy to get me to take my guys in there? Why not be a man and ask me? Better yet, just fuckin' tell me that's how it's gotta be. I wanna go take this guy's heart out myself for him fucking up Jimmy, but not if we're walking into a trap." Joe looked over his shoulder toward the café entrance. "Where the fuck is Alex?"

* * *

The room quieted as Joe walked in on a meeting that was in process in the conference room. On one side of the table sat Joe's team while Pat and Jimmy's team sat on the other.

Sean broke the silence. "How about you clear all this bullshit up, huh, Joe?"

"Going to have to be more specific."

Tim clucked his tongue. "Pat here says he wants us take out a drug lord and his cronies."

"It was discussed earlier," said Joe. "But no decision was made."

Sarge stood up. "We were all there this morning. That group meant to kill us and take our shit. Jimmy is laying in a fucking hospital bed getting stitched up. Jimmy is family. You damn well know that if this happened to one of ya'll it wouldn't be up for discussion."

Sean pointed at Sarge. "So if I'm understanding your logic correctly, you're saying we should seek retribution, potentially risking lives, instead of simply going around the threat?"

Sarge threw a clipboard at the edge of the table. "Fuck all that pussy shit. We deal with him now."

Sean jabbed his finger on the table, saying, "Ain't no pussy, fuckhead. Did I say I wouldn't deal with him? When did I say that? Tell me. You can't, so shut your mouth."

Tim said, "We could roll in there with the loaders and knock the building down while they're in it. We have two of them now, so it wouldn't be too loud and we could roll in at night."

Alex shook his head. "I'm sure they'd have spotters call it in and they'd escape before we got close. We're going to have to be better than that."

"Best thing I can think is to sneak in after zero one hundred," Joe said, "get a look at their base. If the chance arose, maybe we'd take a shot at him, so long as we're comfortable knowing the sound would wake everyone up."

"We don't have any NVGs or suppressors?" said Colton, turning his gaze toward Pat.

"We found four pairs of night vision goggles and two spotter scopes so far on base, which will come in handy. As for suppressors, nothing yet."

Joe raised an eyebrow at Sean. "Might have something for that, but gotta check with my quartermaster."

"Some men just ain't cut out for this shit." Sean placed an open hand on his chest and winked at Joe before turning to Pat. "Breaks my heart."

15

FIFTEEN

June 21

Joe sighed in relief when Sean pushed a cart stacked with suppressed rifles and pistols into the meeting room at the Coast Guard Yard. After he handed them out, the team spent the afternoon shooting and making sure the guns were sighted in for that night.

Having sighted in the rifle, Joe cleaned it then checked his gear before starting the training.

Tensions ran high as Pat led the evolutions on how to work in pairs as a shooter-spotter team.

After a few hours, the six men felt as confident as they could that they were ready.

While Pat debriefed everyone, Joe watched Sean and Ryan from the edge of the building. They were drilling with the convoy on how to approach if the call came. The idea was that, if they got pinned down, they would come in and let one loader wreak havoc while the other covered the MRAP.

It was nearing eighteen hundred hours when they all broke off to go eat in the cafeteria. Everyone ate quietly at a couple of fold up tables when Ryan said, "Shit, you quiet fucks making it feel like this meal is the last supper. We've done all we can to prepare in what time we got. Let God do the rest."

Joe said, "On that note: guys, no heroes tonight. Do your jobs and we all come home."

Sean said, "*Jobs?* A job is where you go to a place you hate and they pay you. No, this shit ain't a job. This is non-profit, save-the-world type shit. Tiny balls need not apply."

"Thought you said it wasn't a job," said Tim.

"It ain't. It's non-profit, save-the—"

"Yeah, yeah, I heard, 'save-the-world type shit,' but then why the talk about need not apply. You apply for jobs, no?"

"I have a few things to go over." Pat squeezed his eyes shut and exhaled, clearly annoyed by the banter. "First, we know from our new friends that some of these guys are former military. We don't know how good their security measures are, but, judging by the waterfront, it's pretty lax. Second, it's a full moon tonight. They will have some visibility, but we have night vision, so we will have an advantage. Lastly, from what we have been told, the guys protecting Shane are assassins. My assumption is that he leaves his B-team on the edges and his guys guard him. So, if you're spotted, take the shot. Hesitation could cost you your life and this whole op."

Tim stood and cased the room, saying, "I know that a lot of these guys won't hesitate to kill us but remember not everyone there is a killer. The people he has his grip on through drugs and coercion, they aren't the bad guys, necessarily. They're survivors like us who've been dealt shittier hands. If someone raises up on you, don't hesitate, obviously, but also don't treat this like we are downrange in some ISIS camp."

Moving from a slouched posture to an upright one, Ryan stared at Tim. "*Damn.* Defending the junkies? Never pictured you to be a tree-hugging braindead liberal."

"I'm not defending them all. Some are pieces of shit. Some will try to kill you for another hit. All I'm saying is, you can't put them all in that category. After getting injured, my brother got prescribed Percocet. And he fell down that hole, too, started buying them illegally for a while. His marriage went to shit, but eventually he got it together and made it out. And like him, most of these people are good folks. Kill more than we need to, you run the risk of making more enemies than you need to."

Joe slapped the table to get everyone's attention. "Good point, Tim. Of course, ultimately, it's up to you and your spotter to decide who is a threat and who isn't. Now let's get some rest and meet at the dock at twenty-three hundred."

* * *

Joe felt like he'd just closed his eyes when a hand shook his foot. It was Jeff from Sarge's team. "Wake up, bud. It's time."

Joe sat up and blinked. "Rock and roll."

Jeff fired up the old Caterpillar diesel on Dell's boat. "Your brother and Sean were asleep as soon as they climbed in the MRAP."

"No surprise there," said Joe. "Both of them are used to sleeping in heavy equipment."

As Joe and Jeff loaded the boat, the MRAP came down the road with the rest of the guys.

The last sliver of the sun peeked above the horizon, shooting reddish hues all across the sky. Joe said, "Red sky at night, sailor's delight."

"Never too late to make it a fishing trip," said Jeff.

"If only."

As night closed in, the rest of the group loaded onto the old deadrise. Jeff set their course and ran at a slow, quiet pace with the lights off. Spencer took his boat past Joe's team and came to a stop out in the channel.

When they pulled toward the coal pier, Joe signaled for everyone to turn on the night vision and start scanning the area.

No sentries.

They hurried up and tied off the old deadrise to the coal pier while Spencer headed into the channel to keep watch and wait for the extract.

Joe loaded a round into the 203 launcher on his M4 and checked the tape on his grenades one last time, then pulled the Walther P22 pistol Sean had given him for the mission.

The group offloaded and scurried up the dock. When they hit land, they split into three teams and headed for their designated locations. Jeff and Colton were to climb up and take position on the roof of the MTA Mobility building across the street from the bar. Tim and Reese were going to setup on the roof of Beltsville Auto Recyclers, farther to the north. Joe and Pat were to take the fire station southwest of their location, which sat across the park from the bar.

While Tim and Jeff took their teams north, Joe and Pat went south toward Benhill Avenue. It was a long run down Benhill to Curtis Avenue. Once Joe and Pat neared the intersection, Jeff radioed in, "Me and Colton are in position. Joe, we aren't going to have a visual of you until you get past the warehouse. We'll keep an eye on the bar and let you know if we see any movement."

Pat replied, "Copy, Jeff. Tim, you close to being in position?"

"Just got to the—back yard of the—the auto recycler," Tim said, his words punctuated by heavy breaths. "Going to take some effort to get up on the roof. Call ya back in—ten—when me and Reese get up and comfortable."

"Gonna have to double time it down this alley, Joe. We got the cleanest shot from the firehouse."

As they ran, Joe found himself thinking about Brooke. She had loved to run. It had never been Joe's favorite activity, but somehow, she'd gotten him to go with her on a number of occasions. He pictured her pony tail swaying back and forth in front of him as his lungs struggled to keep pace.

A hand grabbed and pulled him down behind a dusty Pontiac Bonneville. "What the hell are you doing, son?" Pat hissed. "You planning on walking up and saying hello?"

Joe caught a whiff of a sweet green apple smoke, and rose slowly to peek over the hood of the car when he saw a pair of men leaning against a burned-out car no more than thirty yards away. The bigger of the two had a shiny bald head and a thick beard wrapped around his jaw. He wasn't large per se, but he looked imposing compared to his slender counterpart. The smaller guy held a plastic-tipped cigar and kept shaking his head and taking his free hand on and off his hip while speaking. Joe couldn't make out whatever he was saying.

Pat jerked his head toward an alley leading to Cypress Street and they darted across the street and hid behind an old square-body Ford pickup at the mouth of the alley.

"Straight shot from here to the firehouse," said Joe. "Once we make sure it's clear we will have a good position to see the bar Shane's at."

Pat looked at him with concern, but Joe held his gaze as he said,

"There is a door right alongside the firehouse," said Pat. "Hopefully it's unlocked."

Pat ran halfway down the alley, ducked behind a pair of trash cans, and waved Joe forward. Before Joe could move, they came across the same sentries from earlier. Joe and Pat waited as the men rounded the corner at the far end.

"He's lost his shit." The bald man pulled a joint from his pocket and lit it. "Like some backwater hillbillies would be dumb enough to even try."

"He can be a dumb fuck, that's for sure," said the smaller one. "Running around in the pitch black with these old-ass guns."

They continued to walk, then the larger man stopped several feet in front of where Pat was hiding. The smaller man, a few paces ahead, turned back and asked him what's wrong. The larger man exhaled a cloud and smiled, then held his joint out and remarked how good it was. "You want?"

Pat disappeared in the shadows until the bald man took a few more steps. Pat then slowly stood and unsheathed his knife. He stayed on the balls of his feet as he approached the larger man from behind, grabbed his mouth, and slit the man's throat ear to ear. Pat let the guy drop to his knees. The smaller guy turned around, saw the bald man with his mouth agape and blood gushing through the fingers he held around his own neck. The smaller man yelled, "Fucking shit," and was reaching for the revolver stuffed in his rear waistband when Joe fired three shots in rapid succession. The smaller man joined the bald man on the ground and trembled once before going limp.

After Joe and Pat dragged the bodies behind the trash cans, Joe called to Tim and Jeff to be advised that roving patrols were in the area. Joe squinted at Pat, saying, "Did we really have to kill them?"

"I have no interest in leaving behind a couple of shitbags who can potentially fuck up our whole op. It was a judgment call. Wasn't that what you advised?"

Joe knew it wasn't worth arguing. "Whatever you say, man."

At the end of the alley they stopped and eyed the red door to the firehouse. Joe whispered that he'd go check it out.

When Joe got to the door, he pressed on the thumb latch and tugged. Unlocked.

The door squeaked slightly as he pulled it open, causing Joe to pause.

No movement.

Joe took one step inside when a man rushed at him with a pipe in hand. Joe reached for his pistol and the man's eye socket imploded as he heard the slide action from the pistol.

Standing behind Joe, Pat said, "Should we have saved him, too?"

Under his breath Joe called Pat a dickhead and ran into the first floor of the firehouse, pressed his back against the side of a fire truck, and surveyed the room. The first floor was barely big enough to fit the fire truck and the few rows of turnout gear. Once Pat joined him, Joe started a trip around the truck to ensure no one else was there.

Joe returned to where Pat stood and pointed to a small wooden staircase in the corner.

They crept up to the second floor, where they remained in the shadows on the stairs. They found four middle-aged males, dressed in fatigues and clean-shaven, sitting around a candlelit table playing cards while an iPod played through a pair of fist-sized speakers in the corner. The two men who were closest had sidearms. Joe also spotted several AR15s laying on the ground beside the table.

Joe and Pat crouched there for a minute to get a feel for them.

The guy closest to the steps said, "Fuck it, suppose Shane's right. It'd be nice to see some action outside of the typical mouthbreathing dead. Make Swiss cheese out of rednecks."

Pat raised an eyebrow and Joe feigned indifference. Pat pointed to the two on the right and then back to himself. He pointed to the two on the left for Joe. As Pat took a step, the floor creaked, and the man closest turned and squinted. His eyes grew wide and one of the others said, "Took you long enough, Princess. Come on, your deal."

Pat fired four shots from the .22 and Joe fired six from his pistol. Three of the four men dropped. One of Joe's targets lunged for an AR15 and Pat fired two rounds into him where he fell across the table, knocking the drinks and some of the cards off it.

Joe strode to a window overlooking the park and club. "I'll secure the door and make sure the bay door's locked. Call the guys, tell 'em we made it."

Downstairs, Joe found some rope in a rescue bag. He tied one end to the door lever and the other to the bumper of the fire truck. He checked the fire truck, found keys in the ignition. He turned them and the panels lit up, then turned the engine off and ran back upstairs.

Pat had moved two chairs to the window and had his night vision on so he could scan with his spotter scope.

"Couple guys down by the park," Pat said. "And a few across the street by the wall."

"How about the buildings around here?"

"Nothing visible."

Joe radioed Tim and Jeff. "You guys see anyone posted in the surrounding buildings?"

Jeff said, "Saw an old woman above the park look out her window. That's about it."

Tim said, "One in the building east of you. Don't appear to be too concerned about lookout work though. Been milking a bottle of whiskey at least since we got up here. What now?"

"Now? Now, we wait," Pat said. "He'll come out of that bar. Could be tonight, could be tomorrow morning. He'll show his face sooner or later."

From the window, Joe scanned the area outside as he talked to Pat. "They told me at work this used to be a great neighborhood years ago. Still seems the same even with the world falling to shit."

Pat glanced up and smiled. "Yeah, so was Iran, but I wouldn't want to go there now."

Joe felt his eyes roll like Cara's had done to him so many times before. "Except this place isn't halfway around the world."

Pat's nose made a sound as he exhaled hard. "Maybe some day."

Joe yawned. "Probably gonna be here all night. No chance this asshole will do us a favor and pop out right now."

"I'll take the first watch," said Pat. "You're probably tired, judging by earlier."

Joe swayed back slightly. "How's that?"

"The alley. You seemed a bit out of it."

"I'm fine. Was thinking about my old life."

"Alex said she passed. Your wife. Was she infected?"

"Does it matter? It changes nothing."

Pat looked back through the scope then back at Joe.

Joe kept his eyes out the window. "I wasn't even suppose to be working that night. Went in for some easy overtime. She always told me I worked too much. That I didn't enjoy life enough." Joe stared at his palms. "She'd always quote that kind of shit. Shame I didn't listen to it instead of just hear it." Joe swallowed spit and let several moments pass. "I don't know. I hate thinking about what ifs."

Pat scratched behind his ear, saying, "Blame yourself long enough and you'll become a shell of who you were. Regardless, you're part of the reason Cara and your family are safer tonight than last. But enough with this backslapping. You'll figure it out. For now, hop in the racks over there and try to lay back. I'll grab you if someone comes."

* * *

Pat shook Joe awake. "We got some movement, get ready."

Joe hopped down and ran to the window. He stretched his eyes as he looked through the scope and saw the man from the truck at Fantasies. He had a small security detail with him. Joe assumed this was Shane. Joe scanned the area and saw a few additional groups fanned out along the park.

His sights back to the guy from the Fantasies parking lot, Joe said, "That guy right there, in the middle. The one with long hair."

Joe keyed the mic on the radio. "Jeff, the middle guy, that's Shane."

Jeff's voice came over the radio. "Understood. We have a clear shot. Say when."

"Negative," said Pat. "We have the shot. When you see him drop, take out his men. Tim, do you have eyes on the situation?"

"We have visual of the sniper in the building and can see the street. After you hit him, we'll take the sniper and any we can who flow out onto the road."

"Aye, aye. Leaving mic open to relay faster. On my mark." Pat took a deep breath and exhaled slowly. As the air ran out of his chest, he squeezed the trigger. The shot hit Shane in the side of the head and he collapsed. It was a small caliber round, so there was no exit. Shane's security detail surrounded him and his other men ran toward him with weapons drawn and searching for the shooter.

The other teams began firing and two men dropped. Jeff called out over the radio, "Shit, dude, these guys are starting to come out from all over, permission to ghost back to the boat?"

"Granted," Pat said. "Start your egress. Tim, hold position and take anyone that goes for Jeff."

Joe was thumbing the 203.

"Hold off on that," Pat told him. "We need to make our way back fast and quietly."

Two of the sentries standing there dropped as loud cracks from Jeff's .308 rang out. The remaining men began firing in Jeff and Colton's direction.

Jeff called out over the radio, "Spencer, we're coming around the coal pile now, have the boys on the boat ready. Prepare for company."

Tim added, "We are going to hold our position until Jeff is clear and then we'll roll out to the secondary extract. Spencer cover Jeff 'til he gets off the pier and head to the secondary extract."

Spencer's voice came over fuzzy, "We'll be there."

Pat leaned his head over while still staring into the scope, causing his neck to crack. "We need to take out the second in command or they'll just reorganize."

A dozen men sprinted out of the club. They looked at the group holding Shane and pointed towards Jeff's previous location. Two men began yelling over Shane's corpse. One of them ran off. Pat shot the one who remained.

Pat turned and looked at Joe. His eyes were wider than usual and had a crazy look that Joe hadn't seen before. "Now."

Joe ran down the stairs and untied the rope. As soon as he finished, the line was pulled out of his hand. He looked up at a dirty man who was missing one of his front teeth. The man turned his rifle on Joe. "You ain't, Eddie."

Joe jumped away from the fire truck and drew his pistol. He felt two rounds hit him in his vest. As Joe slammed into the wall, he took aim and fired five rounds, knocking the man out the door. "We got company!" Joe got into the fire truck and turned the key. The engine whined as it turned over and refused to start. Joe shook the wheel as Pat came down the stairs. "She's out of gas. Gonna have to hoof it."

"We should wait. We'll make some noise while Tim and Reese run to the secondary extract. Once they're out, we can have Sean and Ryan pick us up while Sarge and Matt draw their attention."

Joe pulled the mag and reloaded as Pat called out over the radio, "Everyone get that?"

The radio crackled with acknowledgments.

"You'll get to use that 203, after all," said Pat.

Joe ran upstairs, leaned the rifle back, and let a 203 round go. The round soared and hit the corner of the club, blowing bricks all over the street. Joe reloaded and Pat took the window next to him, laying down anyone who ran toward their location.

Pat hit the mic on the radio, "Tim, are you at the extract?"

Tim responded frantically, "Nope, pinned down behind some train cars. Requesting Spencer meet us by the crane dock north of where we were dropped off."

"We can hold this for a while. I'll go tie the door back off," Joe said. "Send Ryan and Sean to help them."

Pat cued the mic. "Ryan, deploy your guys forward. Plow through the junk yard and find Tim and Reese."

"Almost there. Tell 'em to hold on."

Joe aimed at another man who had wandered out of the club and was walking down the street with his rifle raised. Joe pulled the trigger and the round hit him in his torso, spinning him toward Joe. The man looked up at the window and started firing wildly at the firehouse. The MRAP barreled through the fence, over the man, and into the auto lot.

Tim hit the mic. "We see you guys. Open the fucking door."

A barrage of shots came over the mic and in the distance.

Tim's mic came to life again. "Fuck, fuck, fuck. Joe, I'm hit."

More gunfire.

Joe radioed, "Tim! Tim! Come back, over." Joe leaned down, saw another man race across the field. When he got to the end of the field by a basketball hoop, he stopped. Joe fired two shots, hitting him in the neck with the first one and the rib cage with the second.

Joe radioed again, "Ryan, Sean, are you to Tim yet?"

Sean called in over the radio, saying, "Tim's hit bad. He's down. We're loading him now. Requesting immediate evac to Coast Guard Yard. Need a table ready upon arrival."

Pat responded, "Go, we'll find a way home. Requesting loaders to create a diversion at the club. Once commotion starts, we'll self-extract. Boat teams, drop off your guys and call us when you're on the way back."

Spencer called in over the radio. "Aye, Jeff got hit, too, but not life threatening. We are gonna take them over and we'll be back. Base requesting reload for small arms."

Pat was silent for a moment. "Once the loaders do their thing, we go to the ship yard."

Joe kept his eye on the bar. "Won't work. They blew that covering Jeff. We need to head out through Bloody Pond. Can get up to the highway from there."

"Aye, you're gonna have to lead the way. I don't know that area."

Joe looked up from the scope, said, "Will do," then refocused on the bar, waiting to see if anyone else surfaced.

Once the loaders came into sight, Crazy yelled over the radio, "Somebody call the demolition crew? 'Cause we here now mothafuckas!"

The first loader slammed into the bar, rattling it. As it backed up, the second loader hit the bar near the main entrance. Cracks ran up the building's walls. Both loaders started ramming the adjacent walls, causing the other walls to buckle. A few more hits and the building collapsed. Only the back wall was left standing.

As Crazy and Sarge leveled the building, Joe saw a man run out of a building toward the west.

Joe pulled his rifle up, took aim, but hesitated. Joe lowered his rife and Pat made a noise in his throat, a click. Joe grabbed his pack from the floor and stood up.

While many men blur the lines between killing and murder, for Joe, the difference was clear.

Joe and Pat hurried down the stairs and untied the door. Joe's heart pounded as he swung the door open and stepped back with his pistol drawn. Nobody.

They moved across the street and stopped at the corner. Pat asked Joe which way. Joe said to take the alley until it runs out, then they'd go right and cross the street. Once they cross, they'd take a left and head for the construction company. From there, they could cut through to the woods and follow the trails all the way to 695.

The alley was quiet. Too quiet, really. Joe raced down the alley, worrying as he crossed each street that they would be spotted. At the last street they turned and darted across the last road, holding his breath for a moment trying to hear if anyone had followed them. When they cleared the street he exhaled with relief. They had made it into the woods. When they got a few feet into the brush Joe said to Pat,

"Some time since I've been back here. Long as we keep heading left at any fork, though, we should wind up by the fuel tanks. There we can cut through or follow it around and call in when he hit the highway."

"Maybe," said Pat. "We have night vision and they don't, or so I hope. That in mind, it would be best to stay in the woods."

The trail Joe remembered wasnovergrown with briars and blocked by a few fallen pine trees. As they followed the path they saw a large nine-point buck take off to the south. They crouched down and waited to see if the sound had alarmed anyone. Joe and Pat listened. A squirrel started making the odd pitched alarm to warn the other animals that they were there. An owl called out and from the distance they heard the scream a fox makes. Joe whispered, "Forgot how loud the peace and quiet of nature can be."

It took them a while following the trails, but eventually they found the fuel area. As they neared the edge of the woods, Pat grabbed Joe's shoulder. "Up there. Shooter."

At the top of the tank was a man's silhouette facing their direction. He was staring blindly into the brush. Through the night vision, the stars sparkled like diamonds behind the silhouette. The full moon stared back behind the shooter without a cloud in the sky blocking it. As Joe remained crouched behind the brush with his rifle at the ready, he couldn't help but think about how few stars he had noticed before all the lights went out.

Pat whispered, "Wait for him to turn and we'll move away from here."

Once the silhouette moved out of sight, Joe and Pat followed the fence line toward the highway. Joe kept his head moving back and forth from the ground in front of him to the road up ahead. He could see the hill now as he pushed some sticker bushes out of the way and held them long enough for Pat to take them. They were close. Joe stopped, knelt down, and checked his surroundings. He listened for the sounds of branches breaking, brush being forced through, but there was nothing. As he stood back up and moved, Joe could see the rocky hill that led to the highway. Once they got up there they could lay low and call Ryan in.

Joe leaned his head down and told Pat, "Hill's gonna be slick, watch your feet."

As they neared the top, Pat lost his footing. Joe reeled at how loud the little bit of rock and gravel rolling down the hill was. Joe picked up his pace and made for the top. When he got to the edge of the road he scanned the woods behind them for any movement.

After what felt like an eternity, Pat reached the highway.

They ducked behind some bushes near the start of the bridge and Pat called in. "We're at the highway. How close are you for extraction?"

Ryan said they were close. They had been driving back and forth waiting on them.

Joe told Ryan to look right as he came over the bridge, that he and Pat were just past the fuel tanks, underneath an exit sign.

A couple of minutes ticked by until they heard the humming of the MRAP's tires on the highway. Joe walked to the edge of the road and clicked his flashlight on and off three times.

Ryan pulled up, and Sean swung the door open and said, "Come on, fuckhead. Let's boogie."

As Joe turned to climb in the truck, he shook his head and smiled, telling Sean, "Good to see you, too, asshole." Joe then felt something pinch his back and he heard the loud crack from a rifle. A second shot pierced him in the right thigh. Joe fell forward onto the steps at the back of the MRAP. Sean ran out, grabbed the straps on Joe's plate carrier, and yanked him into the truck. Pat fired his rifle. After a few dozen shots, Pat jumped the guard rail, climbed into the MRAP, and before he had the door closed he was saying, "Drive!"

Ryan made a U-turn in the median, stomped the gas, and headed back for the Coast Guard Yard.

As the MRAP straightened out and picked up speed, Ryan yelled back, "He okay?"

Pat had climbed down and wrapped a tourniquet around Joe's leg and was pulling off his body armor. He pulled up Joe's shirt and saw bruising to the left of his spine, just below the shoulder blade. "He'll be okay. The plate took the brunt of the bullet in his back, but judging by that bruise, I'm guessing he had a 7mm or a 30-06. As for the leg, it only tore through the edge of the thigh. Going to have a limp for a while, but he'll manage."

Joe leaned back and pain coursed through his leg. He winced. "God damn that fucking hurts."

"Language, peckerhead. Be happy." Sean said, "You got your first enemy marksmanship badge."

16

SIXTEEN

June 22

Joe's pants were covered in blood and his legs were concrete. The tourniquet had slowed the bleeding, but blood still trickled down his thigh.

After they passed the Coast Guard Yard's main checkpoint, Joe saw two men, illuminated by the pink sunrise, posted in a mobile tower. The MRAP was parked in front of the medical building. Sean swung the door open. Pat hopped out. Joe leaned forward, put his hand on Pat's shoulder, and slowly climbed down. The weight on his wounded leg hurt like hell, but he limped ahead with Pat and Sean at each side.

When they got inside, a corpsman unrolled a bed, saying, "Doc is working on Tim, so I'm going to patch you up. Get him stripped down."

Sean and Ryan undid Joe's shoes and scissored off his pants. Joe saw the wound in his leg and cringed.

Sean smiled as Ryan squeezed Joe's thigh just below the bullet wound. "You feel this?"

Joe twitched from the pain. "You're fucking dead."

Ryan laughed and tsked. "Tell me something new."

Pat and Ryan helped Joe climbed onto the gurney.

The corpsman rolled Joe down the hall.

"How's Tim doing?" asked Joe.

The corpsman gave a crooked smile. "What's your blood type?"

"O positive."

"Good to know. Once we get you in here, we'll get you a pint readied, too."

"Thanks, doc."

Joe leaned back and wanted to close his eyes, but the pain continued pulsing through his leg. He had his eyes closed for a minute before being startled by the sound of a shutting door. The corpsman and Jeff walked toward Joe.

"Tim?" said Joe.

"The shot in his shoulder went through and luckily didn't hit an artery," said Jeff. "The bullet to his calf is a little worse. Missed the bone, but he suffered damage to his tendons. It should heal, mostly."

Joe took a deep breath and exhaled.

"Now, it's your turn," Jeff said as he loosened the tourniquet.

* * *

When Joe woke up, Cara was laying on his left side. He groaned and wiped the sleep from his eyes. "What time is it?"

Cara looked at her watch. "Almost noon. You okay?"

Joe went to move and pain shot up his leg and back. "I could use something to eat. Have you seen Tim?"

A tear streamed Cara's cheek. "I love you, Daddy."

"I love you, honey. I'm okay. I'll have some cool scars in the future, but otherwise, I'm good." Joe winked at her. "Really. I have to ask, what's this I'm hearing about you going out on missions with Jim Shaw? You know I have to beat the crap out of him now, right?" Joe smiled even though he was half serious.

Cara used the heel of her palm to wipe tears. "What if you don't come home one day? Like, what if I end up alone?"

Joe closed his eyes.

"I'm more fit to do this than most of the old guys you drag around with you," she said.

Joe felt his skin warm as his temper rose in anger. "No more until I get the job done in Baltimore. Afterwards, we can discuss—let's say, some options."

Cara rolled her eyes. "Whatever."

"Cara. Promise me."

"Sure, whatever. Yeah."

Joe shifted his body toward his daughter. "Say the words."

"I promise, *jeez*. Why are we still talking about this?"

Joe carefully removed the IV needle from his hand. He brought his feet around and put them on the ground. Pain flared up in his right thigh. He looked down at himself. A blood-soaked t-shirt and a pair of wrinkled boxer shorts.

"Uncle Alex brought you some clothes," Cara said, pointing to the side table.

"Wait here," Joe said. "Be right back."

Joe set out the clothes and took a towel and hung it over the shower curtain rod. As he stripped down, his boxers grazed the leg where the shot had hit him, causing him to tense up before finishing removing them. As he waited for the water to warm, Joe held onto the railing to ease the weight off his leg. Once the water felt warm he climbed in and showered the best he could, feeling and moving like an old man. He winced at the sight of the bruises on his chest and back.

Cara stood waiting by the door when he returned. She took his hand and they walked down the corridor. They stopped in front of a door with a paper sign that read: SEAFORD, TIM.

Joe opened the door and Tim turned his head toward him.

Joe said, "You had me worried, but then I remembered: you're too stubborn to die."

Tim moaned and smiled through clenched teeth. "Not all of us had a plate to take the brunt of our mistakes."

"Yeah, well, take some time and heal up," said Joe. "Gonna need you down the road."

Tim shook his head. "Gonna be out of commission for a few days. In the meanwhile, perhaps you could find me a prettier nurse."

Cara rolled her eyes. "Gross."

"I'll see what I can do," said Joe. "I know people."

As Joe and Cara left the room, Tim yelled to Joe, "Least make sure she bleaches her mustache."

Joe limped into Pat's new office. Alex and Pat were there studying papers that covered a large oak table.

Alex stretched his good hand out across the desk. "Look who's up and moving. Good. A little PT and you'll be right as rain."

"Cut the shit, Alex." Pointing at the papers strewn all over the table, Joe said, "What's going on?"

"No rest for the weary. Ten-four." Alex stood up from behind the desk. "While you were in recovery, we sent Mister Bull back to his friends in Curtis Bay. We gave him a johnboat and radio." Alex went to the window and pointed out across the water with his amputated arm. "To our surprise, the townies finished the job you guys started. The numbers are a little hazy, but he reported that the few survivors from Chauncey's gang were dealt with. Some of the townies want to work with us on clearing the rest of Baltimore. They'd like to lower the Hanover Street Bridge and move back into the city."

Joe raised his eyebrows as he tried to hold back a laugh. "How do we know this ain't a trap?"

"To be frank, you removed any reason they had to fuck with us. That shooting gallery you all put on, followed by the mayhem your loaders and MRAP did, was a pretty convincing tactic."

Joe walked to a cabinet by the window. On top of it stood a bottle of Bulleit Bourbon. He grabbed two of the glasses and poured a fingers worth into both glasses. He handed one to Alex and said, "Well, *salute.*"

Alex and Joe raised their glasses and downed them in one sip. Joe sat the glass down and took the chair across from the desk. "What now? I know you both have something in mind."

Pat walked around to the edge of the desk. "Now's the time for you to take that promotion, start leading more people than your team. When this all started, the President, under direction of SecDef, put a plan in action to use retired operators and some active duty to relocate back home and establish local militias to battle the infected presence."

Joe kept his gaze on Alex and said, "So, Alex and you were getting info from the same guys and we were just another contingency?"

"Correct. Your meeting with us helped put Alex back in contact with his friends at the DoD and handed your group this area of operation. After last night, and given the vote held by the remaining members of Congress, any acting militia member with prior military service has been reactivated and any member who hasn't will be activated at a proper rank."

Pat walked around and put his hand on Joe's shoulder. "We want you to know that the methods you and your team developed have been shared and used in other theaters across the states with great success. Due to this and the following your group has received, I have been authorized by the SecDef to give you a field promotion to the rank of Captain in the United States Navy."

Joe turned his head up and stared at Pat. "And you?"

Pat hesitated, then smiled as he looked out the window.

For the first time, Joe saw an emotion in Pat he'd never seen in him before. Was it embarrassment? Humility?

"Promoted to Admiral." Pat went to the cabinet and grabbed the bottle of bourbon and opened it. He took a big sip and recorked the bottle. "Once we're done here, you will need to figure out the promotion ranks of your team. Pay will be retroactive upon the country's revival."

Absentmindedly, Joe ran his hands over his head and pushed on his cheeks. "I'm a full bird captain now? That's what you're saying? A fucking captain?"

Pat nodded. "Captain."

"Captain. That sounds nice." Joe told Alex, "After we finish with Baltimore, we'll figure out the logistics. In the meantime, Captain fucking Joe Wylie. Tell all your friends." Joe winked at Alex.

17

SEVENTEEN

June 23

It was nearly noon when Joe arrived at the makeshift auditorium the Coast Guard had set up. More than a hundred people were there waiting anxiously for the meeting to start.

Joe limped to the front of the room where Cara and his team sat. As Joe took his seat, he saw Doctor Jeff wheeling in Tim from the door on the side of the auditorium.

Pat and Captain Trudoe walked onto the stage.

"Has he ever given a short speech?" Cara whispered.

Pat took the microphone and faced the crowd. "A thank you is in order for everyone here today. So, thank you. Now, with that out of the way, onto the meat of it." Pat walked around to the front of the podium and stood there scanning the crowd. "I spoke with the President a few nights ago and he informed me that, after a majority vote, the military has officially authorized an offensive with the use of deadly force on the entirety of the zombie presence."

Pat continued to recount his conversations with the president, then he detailed the next steps.

Joe struggled to absorb the information against the fatigue caused by all the pain meds he was on.

When it came time to announce medals and promotions, Joe's name was called. After he walked down from receiving his medals and field promotion, he couldn't enjoy the moment. People were being eaten alive. Others simply murdered. Anarchy reigned. Baltimore was going to be cratered from a tactical strike on July fourth. Were scientists making headway on a cure?

Joe slipped out of the reception and checked his watch. 14:30. He climbed into the bed of his F250 and lay on his back, getting as comfortable as he could with his bum leg. He reached into his breast pocket and pulled a softpack of Camel's out. Empty. Joe sniffed the pack before he tossed it next to him and stared at the sky above.

18

EIGHTEEN

June 30

A week had passed since the team had taken their new roles. The first few days had brought in a slew of new recruits, more than half of which were veterans. By the week's end, about a hundred new faces were running around the base.

Ryan got the Doorkicker division. This division took doors, did the dirty work during clearance and extractions, and served as door gunners for armored convoys, which Sean was in charge of. Sean's convoys mopped up after the heavy clearance teams went through. The heavy movers were run by Tim during live operations, with Sarge and Crazy Matt acting as his field commanders. Jeff ran gunboats with Jimmy working as his senior enlisted. Christian was the disaster recovery team, in case any vehicles went down during operations.

Things were taking shape but the team going into Baltimore would be smaller than anyone liked.

Joe was the only one who hadn't taken to his new role. His whole job seemed to be about resolving conflicts between the teams, and it felt like every time he got one resolved, three more sprang up. Joe was also having to lean on people he barely knew, which was not his way. Still, the week had gone fairly well, considering the new arrangements. This changed, however, when Alex strolled into Joe's new office at the Coast Guard Yard.

"You don't have any sharp objects over there, do you?" said Alex. "I'd rather not be mauled today."

"I happened to have a hatchet in my top drawer. I'm out of practice, but you're close enough."

Alex smiled.

"Glad you're here, actually." Joe said, "We have to go over some stuff."

"Oh?"

"I figure we have to start hitting downtown in two days if we want to meet the President's request of raising Old Glory on the Fourth. Right? So—"

Pat then walked into the office with Cara and a few guys in tow. As they entered through the doorway, Joe recognized some faces and shouted, "Nicco! What the fuck are you doing here?" Nicco Concera was an old acquaintance. He and Joe had trained Brazilian jiu-jitsu and Muay Thai at the same gym together. Nicco stood at about six feet and was a burly man, weighing close to 285 pounds. Joe knew he worked for the federal government but had no clue what his job was. "And what the fuck?" Joe said, "Is that Charlie Lutz?"

"Sir," said Charlie. "Homeland Security boss Bill Greenwald told us to bring you a small care package. Permission to speak freely?"

Joe went over and shook Nicco's hand before turning his attention to Charlie. "Permission granted, but only if you tell me how you came across this one? Charlie, I thought you hit the mountains?"

Charlie took a couple steps and hugged Joe. "Naw, dude. I stayed at the base with Michelle. Better digs, better security."

"Well, it's fucking great to see you, brother." Joe smiled at Charlie and turned to Nicco, saying, "Okay, shoot."

Nicco walked over and shook his head at Charlie who made a face like a kid who was about to say something that would get him punished. Nicco turned back to Joe and took a deep breath. "First is the elephant in the room. Congratulations on the promotion. The cables we have been getting at Meade made your team out to be superheroes. It wasn't until they said your full name that Charlie and I realized we shared an old friend. Anyway," Nicco continued, "Bill Greenwald was heading up operations at Fort Meade, and by order of the President, wanted an advisor to come help your effort for this little venture. You know, someone to help keep them up to date on things in real time. Then came the issue with Charlie here. He damn near started a brawl when they said I was the only one they wanted to go, so I figured he could be a help and it couldn't hurt to bring him along."

"The gifts," said Charlie. "Wanna see?"

Charlie, Nicco, Pat, Cara, and Joe filed out the front door. Outside sat a pair of Humvees and a camouflage box truck. Nicco slapped Joe on the shoulder and squeezed. "Isn't much, but we figured some food and ammo could go a long way this close heading into Baltimore."

Joe felt himself smiling. "Nicco. Charlie. Thanks for coming. Appreciate it, guys."

On July 1st at 0700, a fleet of heavy equipment waited at the parade grounds. Tim limped over and smacked the tire of the Volvo A45G heavy dump truck. Like the previous trucks, the cab was steel-plated, but the back had some new modifications: The dump bed had been fitted with a steel cap and a half dozen cutouts to shoot from. A turret with a .50 caliber machine gun mounted to it had been fitted in the middle of the dump bed.

Joe noticed the other three dumps had all been similarly outfitted. "You apply for patents for this, Tim?"

"Office was closed when I called," Tim said before he led Joe to a line of six rubber tire loaders, which had been outfitted with steel plating.

"Rock and roll."

Hundreds of troops were lined up and standing at parade rest when Joe and his crew walked up to the front of their formation.

"Attention on deck!" echoed out.

Joe saluted the troops. "At ease. Friends, we are about to embark on our toughest mission to date. A lot of you were in the military before this plague infested our country, while others just recently joined. I thank all of you for being here. Tonight, after taking back the county, we ride to take back Baltimore, to free the survivors left in the city. To start moving toward a world our kids can live in and grow up like we all did.

"It's not going to be easy and some of you may not make it back. That's the job we chose. People will commemorate this day, the day where you all cleared the *first* city. It will be you all who go forward after this and reclaim the suburbs like Dundalk and Columbia as we head forward to clear out Annapolis where John Paul Jones now resides with the new dead.

"All of you have been detailed to one of my lieutenants, so I want you to get with them and get ready because it's time to show these dickheads that we won't back down. We will not give quarter. We will take this country back!"

The group erupted in cheer. As Joe looked back, he saw his team, everyone with their hands in the air. Even Nicco and Charlie.

Joe let the noise subside before shouting, "Dismissed."

19

NINETEEN

July 2

Joe sat in the large Volvo dump truck at the edge of the city and stared down 295 at the graffiti covering the overpass for West Patapsco Avenue. The fence to the old nail company off to his right was starting to gather Zs when he called up Jeff on the private band of his radio. "Jeff, it's Joe. How's it looking down there?"

Jeff's reply was punctuated by weapon fire. "As well—be expected, man. Anything else—you, sir?" His tone hinting at more frustration than respect.

"You getting a lot of company at the harbor?"

"Fuck, yeah. We have—dropping them steady—they keep coming. Hopefully—slow down before your arrival."

Joe glanced at Spencer, who was behind the wheel, and grabbed the other radio. "Gentlemen, it's time."

Spencer lurched the truck onto the road and took position behind the loaders. Christian and Tim were offloading the 973 track loader from the lowboy. Behind them stood Sarge and Crazy in the two rubber tire loaders. Behind them, a dozen Humvees, six LMTVs, and the MRAP with Pat and Alex and Nicco inside.

It was 0900 when Tim had the track loader ready to go. The fences from the nail factory started to bow from the zombies.

Joe called out to the Humvees and the LMTV crews, saying, "Humvee and

LMTV teams open fire on the Zs at the fence. Drivers, keep spaced and await our call before following."

Tim called to his division over the radio. "Gunners, after Captain gets moving, keep at least three blocks behind him."

Joe radioed the Humvee division. "When you hear three blasts from the airhorn, start your follow, engaging any threat that trickles in."

Spencer was fidgeting with the steering wheel as he asked Joe, "Ready?"

Joe saw fear in Spencer's eyes. "Yeah, get her rolling."

The big diesel moaned and the tracks began chewing up route 295. When the convoy entered the city, Joe signaled to Spencer, who gave three blasts on the airhorn. Spencer pulled on the horn and hundreds of Zs raced out of every alley and building toward the convoy.

Tim's loader bucket parted them like a ship's bow. Joe saw Spencer cringe as he hit the first pile of undead.

Joe grabbed the radio. "Ryan, weapons hot. Your A team is clear to fire. Watch my equipment. Sarge, Matt, buckets down. Plow the dickheads off the road as we go."

The first major venue to pass as they entered Baltimore from 295 was the Horseshoe Casino. The tracks and gunfire drew in hundreds of Zs as they rode past the casino's beige concrete façade and smashed windows. They had climbed an overpass when Joe radioed Tim, saying how they were stacking up behind him. "Humvee teams fall back. We need to thin the herd before they become too many."

"Oh boy," said Tim. "Roger that."

As Tim came down the overpass to where the two Baltimore stadiums sat, he radioed Joe. "Slight change of plans. We'll make a lap around Ravens Stadium to gather 'em up. We don't knock down this pile and give the stragglers a chance to catch up, it's gonna give us real problems."

"Let's you and I break right at the stadium, Matt and Sarge break left. We'll meet up on the backside by the light rail station, then we get back on track." Joe radioed Jeff, "We're hitting some big pockets down here, be a few minutes late. How's the harbor?"

Charlie Lutz replied though Joe couldn't tell if his voice was excited or frantic. "Shit's definitely getting overrun. Practically drowning each other trying to get us."

Tim and Joe neared the light rail station, spotting the rest of the convoy barreling toward them with a mob of Zs close behind. Joe called for them to split, and when they did, the Zs that didn't move quickly enough were met with the 973 bucket or the tires of the big Volvo.

* * *

It was around noon when Joe called out, "Fuel check. Everyone good?" Responses indicated most vehicles stood at about three-quarters of a tank.

Joe called out to the Humvee groups to begin entry, two wide, into the city as rehearsed. "Keep weapons hot and exit routes clear." Joe said, "Don't bunch up."

The turn onto Pratt Street had proven to be more of a pain in the dick than Joe had hoped. The road was crammed with abandoned vehicles. Sarge and Matt had advanced ahead to clear the main road with Tim, while Spencer and Joe idled at the intersection.

As Joe waited for the roads to be cleared so they could advance to the harbor, Ryan's team in the back of the rock truck began firing erratically. Ryan's voice came in muffled over the sound of gunfire, "Big incom—nine—lock!"

Out the driver side window Joe saw a couple hundred Zs racing toward the rock truck. Many were trampling over each other. Joe radioed, "Tim, double time it back here. Need help."

"On the way," Tim said, "hang tight."

By the time Tim finished responding, the Zs had closed the gap and slammed into the side of the rock truck. The truck twitched as they began climbing, piling on top of each other trying to get to Ryan's team.

Joe yelled to Spencer, "Get her moving, now!"

Spencer jerked the wheel. This caused the articulating body to jar, sending a few of the Zs on top of the pile flying. Spencer hit the gas and the rock truck inched forward to the sound of shrieks. As it accelerated, the bed started to teeter to Joe's side of the truck. Joe yelled for Spencer to stop. The bodies were stacked too high under the wheel. They needed to back up or they'd risk tipping Ryan's guys over.

Spencer put it in reverse and cut the wheel. A large male Z sprang onto the driver side door and punched at the small glass window. By the third hit, the glass had cracked. Spencer looked over at Joe with wide eyes.

"Sit back!" Joe drew the pistol from his hip and leaned over close the window. Spencer pushed himself into his seat as much as he could before Joe fired two rounds through the window. Glass shattered outwards and the Z fell from the truck. Spencer cut the wheel, continued backing up. Tim, Sarge, and Matt were coming up the road. With the Zs piling up again against the cab, Joe told Spencer not to stop, to keep her moving unless he wants them coming through the window he just shot out.

Spencer put the truck into gear and it jumped forward. Tim blew past plowing into the pile of Zs. Spencer slammed into a parked car on the passenger side. The cab tilted to the left as the rear tilted, going over the Zs that Tim had run over. Spencer turned the wheel hard left and felt the cab start to go too far over. Joe grabbed onto the door arm to prevent himself from falling into Spencer.

The cab was starting to correct itself when Joe glimpsed a Z in the mirror. With no time to warn Spencer, Joe pulled his pistol and pressed himself against the dashboard as the Z came to the window. The Z reached for Spencer and Joe shot three rounds off, sending it tumbling off the truck as the truck landed down hard on the front passenger tire. Spencer floored it and gave some space for the loaders to plow the road, saying, "Fuck, man. What the fuck?"

"Good job driving, brother."

Spencer breathed in and out, in and out. "Not out of the woods yet."

Joe radioed Tim, told him to get back up front and to keep clearing a path to the harbor. He called out to Jeff and Alex, "Status updates."

Alex answered first, saying there was some small presence and he'd update Joe if the situation changed. Charlie Lutz called in for Jeff and said how there were still a shit ton near him, but he'd hold it down until reinforcements arrived.

When Spencer and Joe neared the Inner Harbor, Joe tried to ignore the wreckage alongside the roads, the broken glass. He tried to ignore the half-eaten bodies and random dog parts and deer strewn about. Joe called out on the radio, "Jeff, we're making our first pass down the strip. Check fire till we're clear."

"Check fire," said Jeff. "Aye."

Spencer wiped the sweat from his brow and pulled his hat back on as he drove past the old fountain and a horde of Zs piled up by the water. "Tim was right… There's a fine line between bravery and stupidity."

Joe radioed, "Everyone. Stay tight to the building's edge. Don't want to see anyone swimming."

Spencer turned and scowled. "Thanks, Dad."

The Volvo bounced down the flight of stairs on the corner of the harbor as Tim pushed the Zs into the water, most of which were already *dead* dead. As for the rest, Zs couldn't swim for shit.

While the loaders pushed along the harbor toward the Science Center, Charlie called out over the radio that Joe had a ton of Zs coming from the east. "Do you want us to engage them?"

Joe sat for a moment to think.

Spencer turned off the path that lead to the Science Center and went back onto the road.

"Charlie, have Jeff engage them and draw them away from us." Joe said, "Bunch them up and frag 'em! Can always clear them up later."

Joe listened to the bursts of gunfire that came from the boat teams. As Spencer followed behind Tim and the other loaders, Joe looked out at the harbor. "One more pass and they should have it cleaned up."

Spencer said, "What?"

"Nothing, just keep her rolling."

As they came back again for another pass the boom from the 203 rounds confirmed that they had killed off most of the threat and were headed to Fort McHenry. Joe lit a cigarette and told Spencer that they have to get the area cleared up and call in the fuel detail.

* * *

It was slightly after five o'clock when Tim called out, "Fueled up and ready to go, Cap."

As Joe, Tim, Sarge, and Matt pulled onto Key Highway, they saw a cluster of Zs heading toward them. The trickle had remained steady during fueling but, with the help of the Humvee teams, it had been done without incident. Tim was out ahead with Sarge and Matt when Joe heard Tim's call come over the radio. "Game faces. We got company, boys."

Radio communications relayed that Zs came in from all over as Tim made his initial impact on the crowd. Tim's track loader cut through them like a hot knife through butter.

Spencer kept the rock truck back as Sarge and Matt swung wide behind Tim to make impact with the wake of bodies. After a few hundred feet of impact, they had filled the buckets with zombies and were plowing the road as they followed.

The convoy continued down Key Highway and Joe saw the sign for the Harris Teeter grocery store. "Sarge, Matt, drop back. Tim, hard left, now!"

Tim's voice sounded unsure as he replied, "Through that block wall? Serious?"

Joe nodded as he hit the button on the walkie. "Yup, here is good. Guys, hold back until we have a clear path."

Joe watched smoke billow from the stack as Tim raised the throttle moments before he slammed the 973 into the wall, taking out the top half of it. Tim backed up and hit it a second time, removing most of the block from the bottom. He lowered the loader's bucket and piled the block up in the bucket as the 973 chugged forwards.

Tim went out of sight to dump the last of the block. Seconds passed before he called Joe. "Company inbound. Lots of company."

Sarge and Matt raced through to help Tim.

Joe waved Spencer forward and radioed Alex to slow down. "Locust Point has a big pocket. We will call when we get it knocked down."

The Volvo moaned as it climbed up the small hill where the block had been giving Joe view of Tim in the loader. Hundreds of Zs charged toward the loader. Tim had the bucket still in the air. When the Zs came in range, Tim slammed the bucket down onto the first wave and the bucket stayed down. "Joe, we got a problem. Hydraulic line blown and losing oil fast."

Before Joe could answer, Crazy Matt called in, "Yeah, mang, we got you. Back her up and we'll take care of the rest."

Joe told Tim to back her up and plug the hole they made, then shut her down so they don't tear her up.

Alex's voice cut in. "Be advised: We will turn at McHenry Row, so focus any gunfire away. ETA five minutes."

Tim backed the loader up as Sarge and Crazy Matt picked up the bulk of the remaining Zs and lured them away around the corner. When Tim passed them, Joe told Spencer to start backing down to get him. Gunfire off the block walls echoed into the cab as Ryan restarted firing from the bed of the Volvo on the Zs that weren't lured away.

When Tim got the 973 parked, he called Joe to see if he was clear to move. Joe saw no Zs in sight. "Ryan, you see any?"

Ryan said there were a few on the opposite side.

"I'll take that as a clear. Make room."

Tim limped down from the cab with his rifle and vest on. The limp would've been worse if not for the adrenaline. Joe was watching Tim from the back of the truck when Spencer yelled on the radio, "Out front, almost to the cab."

Six more Zs came racing around the building, headed straight for Tim. Spencer pointed the Benelli shotgun out the broken window and Joe swung the door open and climbed out on the cab. He took aim and fired away. The first Z fell but the others were almost to the cab. Joe knew Ryan's team was focused on getting Tim in by now, so he fired the rest of his mag and dropped it as he reloaded. There were only two left when Tim called out, "I'm in."

Joe jumped back in and slammed the door as he wedged himself into the corner of the cab. Spencer started rolling the rock hauler around to the parking lot with the sound of erratic gunfire off in the distance. Joe keyed the mic, "All units, where is the heavy fire coming from?"

After twenty seconds of silence, Alex responded, "Key Highway farther away from us. Drone footage was a bit off and we are being chased by a horde. Need immediate assistance. Numbering in the thousands and trailing us. We've picked up speed and are nearing the turnoff. Be there in two."

"Roger that," Joe said, making an effort to keep his voice steady and calm. "Sarge, you and Crazy double back and block the way after the MRAP carrying the Admiral makes her way through. Buckets up and crush all that try to get through. Spencer and I will double back on Key Highway East."

The ride felt like an eternity in the big dump truck. When they passed Matt and Sarge to turn back onto Key Highway, Joe saw the huge group behind the convoy. The last Humvee in the convoy was flipped on its side, and the driver was still firing through the windshield as the passenger was being ripped out by the pack of Zs. Joe radioed the convoy. "Speed up past and turn in. We'll take care of this until you can regroup. Jeff, I need you by Rash Field. ASAP."

Jeff radioed, "Heading there now. Hammer down, Cap."

Spencer asked Joe, "Bravery or stupidity?"

Joe pointed past the wrecked Humvee. "Drive full speed through the crowd and we keep rolling till we get to the turnaround at the harbor."

"We're dancing on that line."

"It's the best option with the 973 down. We're the only chance the guys in that truck have. So, punch it."

Spencer got the rock truck up to speed just as they made contact with front of the pack. The hit slowed them momentarily and allowed a Z ample time to climb up onto the cab. Joe drew his pistol and fired. The bullet hit the Z and it lost its balance and fell off.

Spencer white knuckled the wheel and floored the gas.

The truck finally broke through the zombie swarm. Spencer and Joe high-fived. The plan hadn't gotten them killed. Spencer howled. Then Alex called in to Joe, saying, "You managed to pull most of them off, but the Humvee is lost. No survivors. We still have a long tail chasing us. Matt and Sarge are doing their best to run them down as we engage them. Do what you can with your pack until we clear this and call you back."

"Aye aye. We'll lead them back to Rash Field and make the turnaround there." Joe looked in the mirror at the mass of Zs chasing them and hit the mic again. "From what I'm seeing we took the bulk. Jeff, we are thirty seconds out. You in position?"

Charlie Lutz said no, they were almost at the restaurant.

"Okay, get in position. We can make it work." Joe said, "Spence, speed past the park and we can double back to them right past the Science Center. Hopefully that'll buy 'em enough time."

Spencer got the hauler turned around and was heading along the harbor toward Rash Field when the radio went off. "Joe, man, it's Jeff. We see you."

"Aye, aye. Coming your way. Once we pass light 'em up!"

Spencer sped up after he rounded the tight corner and headed past the field. Joe looked back and saw that they had regained some of the distance they lost on the turnaround, hearing the sound of gunfire from the back of the truck and on the water.

When they got to the end of Rash field, Joe felt the blast from the 203 rounds hitting the pack. It caused the Zs to scatter but the majority hadn't faltered in their drive. After the 203s, the harbor echoed with the sound from the 240 from the boat.

The radio crackled with Charlie's voice. "We knocked down a bunch of them, but we are going to need a second pass. Jimmy's bringing me more ammo. We maybe have enough for one more pass. Try and loop it again and we'll get what we can."

"That's a big ten-four. Let's make it count," Joe replied.

The second pass dwindled the pack to a few hundred as Joe and Spencer headed back toward the rest of the group. When they got in sight of the turn off, Sarge and Crazy flew onto the highway and looped past them to take out the remaining threat.

Joe called in to Alex. "Pack is down. Need to isolate the entrances here, get fuel, reload, and secure the area before nightfall."

20

TWENTY

July 3

Although they had isolated Locust Point the best they could, the gunfire and light continued to draw in more Zs.

It was getting late when Joe ordered everyone to try and cycle in and out to get some rest in the Humvees while others stood watch.

Joe climbed out of the cab, walked over to the MRAP and rapped twice on the back door. Alex opened the door, tried to smile. "Eye in the sky is seeing no major signatures within five miles. Only a few still roaming this area."

Joe yawned and rubbed his eyes. "Good. Not sure these guys would make it through another big attack tonight."

"How you figure?" said Pat. "We did well for what we had. Damn well, in fact."

Joe narrowed his eyes. "By my tally, we lost four people."

"What we did today, and will finish tomorrow, will prevent the city from becoming rubble and ash. So yes, we lost *four* people, Joe, but how many are we going to save?"

"I guess you and I operate under a different calculus."

"Sometimes you have to cut down a few trees to make a cabin."

Joe folded his arms across his chest. "Are you trying to push me?"

"I don't know what you're getting at, but listen: We have some time, right now, tonight, and there's one building left between here and the fort I'd like to check out." Pat raised his eyebrows to Joe. "It could have survivors." Pat said, "Nicco? What say you?"

Nicco peeked over from a laptop. "Survivors? If anywhere, definitely going to be that warehouse. It was a supply warehouse for ships. I'm guessing either most of the locals ran there and so we'll find a group of well-fed people living in a homeless style community, or we have a giant zombie funhouse."

Alex spun around and said, "What type of stuff is stored in a supply warehouse?"

Joe exhaled loudly. "If it's anything like the supply ships, then everything. Food, oil, paint. Shit, you name it, they have it. Or had it."

Pat said, "Problem with that is you're talking about not only a potential fire hazard, but also a well-fed zombie hazard if the place is full of them. We'll need to send a team for recon before we bother deploying our salvage units."

Joe nodded. "Myself and a four-man team would be sufficient."

Alex said, "Who'd you have in mind?"

Joe sat quietly for a minute, then said, "Sean, Colton, Reese. Ryan. They are all in the back of the Volvo, sacked out as we speak. They should be able to get in and out quickly enough to get the job done."

Everyone was in agreement when Joe left the MRAP and walked back to the rock hauler, climbed up to the fabricated truck cap, and tapped on the back door. "Ryan, got a special assignment you."

Ryan climbed down and yawned. "You may be Captain, but you better not ask me to bring kneepads."

"First off, kneepads are for pussies. Second, you, me, Sean, Colton and Reese—I want you guys to go to the warehouse up there and do a threat assessment before morning. If the place is crawling with Zs, we'll need to come up with a plan. If the place is loaded with survivors, I don't want to leave them hanging any longer than we have to."

Ryan wiped the sleep from his eyes. "Let me think about it."

"Don't be a bitch. You got thirty minutes to be loaded and ready to go. I'll grab a Humvee, gunner, and a driver for you."

Ryan half-ass saluted. "We'll be ready."

Joe saluted back. "Okay, bro. Wheels up in thirty."

Joe wrangled one of the drivers and turret gunners on watch, then climbed back in the MRAP. "I got four of mine going with me. We leave in twenty. Let's hope the place is empty and full of cold beer."

While staring off in the distance, Alex said, "God, I'd kill for a Flying Dog right now. Even warm. I'd murder for a *warm* beer."

Joe smiled. "A few bars and liquor stores around this area. We finish this op, I'll personally go find you a sixer of that yuppie bullshit."

* * *

The warehouse was a four-story square building. The water-stained gray paint was faded and soot-covered from years of neglect. The left side of the building had a fire escape from the roof and third floor. Ryan scurried up its ladder and exited on the third floor, positioning himself by the window to wait for Joe, Sean, Colton and Reese to follow.

After a few minutes, the men readied themselves to enter through a door that lead to a catwalk. They listened for anything that might sound like people, alive or undead, but heard nothing. Ryan whispered to the others, "Either they're all former librarians or nobody's home."

Sean waved two fingers in a circular motion. "Let's climb in and take a peek. It may be a good supply of stores."

"No doubt," said Colton. "Best go get a bead on this place so we can let the Admiral know what's what."

Joe nodded and made a knife hand that pointed toward the door. As they walked in, they put on the night vision goggles attached to their helmets and turned them on. The warehouse lit up in a pale green hue, allowing them to see the enormous warehouse from above a large indoor bridge crane. As they moved forward Joe reached out and knocked down the large spiderwebs that covered a section of the catwalk. As he looked down below the catwalk, the only movement that came into view was a large rat racing from pallet to pallet.

They crept forward until they got to where the catwalk split in two directions. Joe pointed to Colton and Reese to follow the path that continued straight down the wall. He pointed at Ryan and signaled for him to hold, then signaled Sean to follow him.

As Joe and Sean reached the far wall, Reese's voice came in over the earpiece. "We have a couple survivors over here on the far corner of the catwalk. Looks like a mother and her kids. Three survivors, asleep. How should we approach?"

Ryan answered before Joe could. "Carefully. They might not be survivors."

"Copy that. Will approach with caution. Will check back in after we know the status of the family."

As they drew closer to the end of the catwalk, Sean stopped abruptly. "Dude, I think we found the remaining citizens of Locust Point."

Overwhelmed by what appeared to be hundreds of Zs piled up near the corner sleeping, Joe stood motionless before he scanned the room and took inventory of what was down there. When he got to the doors, he noticed someone had chained them up from the inside. Before he could finish his scope of the area, Sean tapped him on the shoulder and whispered that most likely the stores had been thoroughly thrashed before everyone went full on Z. Sean pointed to the ground level at a rows of stacked pallets and said how in the middle was a large pallet of flour. "I brought some of my old man's dynamite and one piece of the C-4 he had in my pack. You work on getting the woman and her kids out and I'll drop the dynamite into that pallet of flour. Once it blows, I'll toss the C-4 into it and let it blow. The secondary blast should cause the flour to ignite, flash frying every one of those fuckers."

"Why not drop them with the rifles? Or toss the charge into the heart of the pile?"

Sean shook his head. "Less chance of survivors this way. Besides, once I blow that flour, they'll charge the sound and be incinerated by the blast. Saves ammo, plus gives me payback for—"

Joe doubted the plan as he put his hand up, silencing Sean. "Colton, Reese, sitrep on the woman and kids?"

"Alive. A bit malnourished. Bringing them out to the entrance now."

"Ten-four, get them to the Humvee. Sean has a solution for the dickheads below."

Minutes passed before Reese called in that they were clear. Sean nodded at Joe and headed down the catwalk toward a sleeping pile of Zs. Joe crouched and began sweeping the area one last time before Sean got into position. As he looked down, he noticed off to the east of the sleeping pile stood a stack of propane cylinders. He called Sean on the radio, saying, "Sean, we have an issue east of the catwalk."

Sean surveyed the area. "Even better. I'll place the C-4 in the bottle stack, then blow it after the flour goes up from the dynamite."

Joe's stomach turned thinking about it. "I don't know, man. Seems like too much of a risk. You fall and hit that detonator, we go up with 'em."

Sean turned to look at Joe and smiled. "Nope, got a dummy proof on it." Sean pulled a small cylinder out of his left breast pocket and flashed it to Ryan. It was crudely built, nothing like one of the cool detonators in the movies, but the top had a small switch cover sitting on it to prevent accidental hits.

Joe shook his head. "If you say so."

Sean crept down the catwalk when he heard the creak of the catwalk howl below his feet. He was a few feet away from the propane tanks when the catwalk began to buckle. He grabbed the rail tightly and took a deep breath. Nothing moved. He held on for another second, surprised that the sound had not woken the slumber party below. Sean took another deep breath and eased his grasp of the railing as he went to take the last few steps. Once the charge was set, it wouldn't matter how much noise he made.

Sean took a knee, reached in the bag, pulled out a rectangular piece of C-4 with a small detonator on it. He tied a piece of cord from his pack to it and set the detonator switch on the C-4 before he started lowering it. As he lowered it, he swung it lightly until it fell between two stacks of propane bottles near the center of the pile. He stood, turned to Joe, and gave him the thumbs up. Sean then stopped and called in to Alex and Pat. "Admiral, it's Sean. Shit's about to get a little loud. But the payoff is bullets saved."

Joe cringed when he heard Alex's response. "The fuck you mean it's about to get loud?"

"Place is crawling with Zs and they had barred themselves in before the infection got them. Now we make them go kablooey."

175

Joe looked at his watch. 02:00. "Okay, Sean," he radioed. "Team prepare egress and get enough distance before we blow it."

"Aye aye, Captain." Sean walked along the catwalk and pulled the dynamite from his pack. He grabbed a lighter from his pocket and stood facing the rail. With the pallets of flour below him, he lit the long fuse. The fuse flashed brightly as he tossed it down in between the pallets. The stick hit the ground and rolled underneath one of the pallets. He smiled and waved to Joe, making a shaka hand gesture.

Joe waved Sean to hurry up.

Sean grabbed the detonator and moved quickly toward the exit. As he hit the area where the catwalk had let out the groan earlier, the metal beneath his feet gave way and Sean dove toward the rail and wrapped his free arm around it, holding tightly as the entire catwalk swung down, held up by two small sections of rusted steel. Sean threw his leg around the rail.

"Sean, get the fuck out of there!"

Sean's response was calm. "You first, fuckhead."

Joe felt frozen.

"Seriously, man. *Go.* Get the fuck out of here before we're both dead." Sean said, "Til Valhalla."

Joe's eyes began to water as he turned to run.

At the bottom of the ladder he ran toward the Humvee and said, "Damnit, Sean. Goddamnit."

The explosive went off, followed by a secondary blast which Joe knew was Sean blowing the propane cylinders and filling the room with fire. Ryan watched from the turret as the building blew out in all four directions in a huge explosion. Joe wiped a tear from his cheek as he heard Ryan say, "That crazy ass motherfucker."

Outside in the MRAP, Joe sat and stared at the black heaps of smoke coming from the warehouse fire off in the distance. He shook his head in disbelief and slowly took a knee. He bowed his head, said a short prayer for Sean, then got back inside and sat quietly. The men looked at Joe but said nothing.

About ten minutes had passed when one of the troops knocked on the door. Alex opened it and talked to him briefly before taking a small box before closing the door. Alex handed the box to Joe. "The Humvee driver said this was Sean's. He didn't know what to do with it and I figure he would have wanted you to have it."

Joe opened the box. Inside were driver's licenses, a few ears, several fingers. Joe cringed, felt repulsed as he thumbed through it. He shut its lid and ran his index finger over the box's wooden lid where over a hundred notches had been carved into it just below a small inscription: "For J, J + D." Joe gave the box to Pat. "This should be taken back to the VFW and buried at James' grave. Sean finished his mission for retribution."

"Explains where he was going all those evenings."

"He always said if he had to die, it better be a glorious death." Joe flattened his lips as he nodded. He blinked methodically. His nose twitched. His eyes grew wet.

Quietly, to himself really, Joe said, "Balls of steel."

21

TWENTY-ONE

July 4

Spencer woke Joe from a nap. The couple hours of sleep were not enough. Joe found his resolve in the words he muttered, "Today we finish what we started."

Joe climbed down from the cab and headed to the MRAP with Spencer. He passed by a group of guys who stopped talking as he neared. They all stood at attention and saluted. Joe returned the salute and walked onward. His bloodshot eyes. His tight jaw. The stubble dotting his cheeks and neck. Sean's death weighed heavily on him and his face gave it away.

Joe opened the door to the MRAP. Pat stood and motioned outside. Joe stepped back down and sat on the bottom step and lit a cigarette. As he pulled the first puff, Pat sat next to him.

Joe raised his hand before Pat could speak. "I'm fine. Save that shit for tomorrow, if you must."

"I wish that was it."

"What now?"

"We have a large group of Zs downtown that one of the trucks spotted this morning while bringing in more ammunition and supplies. They are trailing them here as we speak."

"Are you fucking serious?" Joe snapped. "Why didn't you wake me earlier?"

"Just heard about it or I would have."

Joe grabbed the radio from Spencer. "All hands meet at the MRAP who aren't on watch. The rest keep comms clear. Move ASAP."

As everyone gathered, Joe sketched out a plan.

Joe tried to roll the tension out of his shoulders as he watched his lieutenants and the rest of his troops scurry away for their vehicles. As everyone continued to load up he called Jeff to confirm his boat teams were standing by on the southeastern shore of Fort McHenry.

Joe called the convoy. "Convoy, report."

The response was muffled from the sound of gunfire that echoed from the distance. "Captain, we are passing the Science Center now. ETA 5 minutes. Infected presence trailing, numbering in the thousands. Over."

"Peddle down, come straight to the south side of the fort. We will be ready."

Joe's team was in position when he saw the LMTVs round the corner. He called them on the radio as they sped down the service road. "All right, boys. Floor it past us and take position. Team open fire in ten, nine, eight, seven, six—"

Gunfire erupted from all around. The 240s on the boats and fire from the Humvees dropped wave after wave, but the Zs were gaining ground. They were now only a hundred yards away from his team and more than half were still upright.

Joe yelled out over the mic as he opened the 203 launcher, saying, "Fire, fire, fire. Our fucking lives depend on it." Joe dropped an HE round into the tube of his launcher, took aim, and blast off. The subsequent explosion blew dozens of Zs into the air. More kept coming, reaching close enough that Joe could see the redness of their once white eyes.

Gunfire continued from all sides. The thump of grenade launchers, the tone of the M240s joined by the erratic beat of the M4s, it was a symphony of destruction.

Joe reloaded, fired another HE round. Dirt blew out from all over as more Zs fell.

When the remaining few hundred got too close, Joe jumped into the cab with Spencer. "Convoy, move now! Jeff, keep firing. Gotta slow them down." Joe told Spencer, "When they get out front, spin this bitch around and plow through them. Splitting the pack might give us a better chance." Joe called Ryan inside the box from the radio. "When we make this pass, soon as you see them, mag dump into the crowd all the way through."

"You got it, bro."

When the team had pulled far enough away, Spencer made the U-turn. Joe swung open the window and loaded the last 203 round into the launcher. When they finished the turn and were heading straight into the horde, he raised the barrel and let the round fly. It hit the pack's right flank, causing part of it to break off just before Spencer made impact. Joe rested his rifle on the window. Due to the unsteady bouncing inside the cab, Joe was firing wildly into the crowd. With such a large group, however, few bullets missed as Spencer floored it and broke through the ranks while from the bed Ryan's team dumped as much ammo as they could into the ones that had missed the hauler.

When they came out of the other side, Jeff's team came to life shooting into the pack.

Joe felt his pulse beat in his neck. "Again. Same thing." Joe stuck a cigarette between his lips and changed his mag.

22

TWENTY-TWO

August 4

A month had passed since the day that Joe and his team raised the flag at Fort McHenry, turning the tide in the city. In the end, the lives lost helped stopped the planned bombing of Baltimore and led to freeing thousands of survivors.

After three weeks, Baltimore had been given a "Green Zone status" by Pat.

On the last day in Baltimore, Joe had told his team to take some time off and meet at his house for a party a week later. "Mandatory fun, dickheads."

The day of the party, Joe stood on his driveway and felt good, light on his feet. He saw Tim accompanied by Christian who was carrying two bushels of crabs. "Need a hand?"

"No, we got it. So long as you got everything ready to start cooking."

Joe motioned toward the garage. "Propane, beer, and vinegar."

Tim set the crabs down and bearhugged Joe. "Where you been hiding?"

"I've been here. You? You staying on, going to build more Marvin mobiles?"

Tim laughed. "They came calling a few days ago. Told them I'm medically retired. What did you tell them? I'm sure they been down here, not to mention their number one recruiter lives with you."

"Who, Alex? He hasn't been here much. He and Pat have Cara working with them and I'd bet the farm Cara told them to leave me alone for a week. Alex and I talked, but he hasn't brought it up, just asked how I'm doing."

"Lucky you." Spencer tossed a few crabs into the pot. "He has stopped me three times already at the VFW. Two nights ago, I told him that I would stay on only if he left me alone. My guess is he's gonna drag Pat down to strong arm you into staying on as the big chief."

"He better bring someone better than Pat." Joe grabbed a lawn chair. When he sat down he smiled. "Maybe if he brought Jennifer Aniston I would be more inclined."

"Sheeit," said Tim. "You did good but, you ain't that good."

Joe smiled. It had been too long since he had enjoyed a conversation. That, and they'd *done* it. They'd fucking done it. But what would it be this time? Where was the next threat? The thought extinguished Joe's smile.

Tim slapped Joe on the back and said, "Who knows, though, we are famous. So, if he wants you, he is gonna bring a big gun since you have some authority to tell him to fuck off."

While the men talked, Charlie walked into the garage. Spencer handed Charlie a beer and Charlie said, "Joe, my man, you know you want to, admit it. No way your ego could let someone else do it. We could take these deadrises all the way to Barbados. You can't tell me you don't want in on that."

"With winter just around the corner," said Joe, "they'll probably go north to clear out New York and Jersey."

"Fuck that. Overrated pizza and America's armpit? We're gonna go south. Pat promised."

"Okay, that and fifty cents might get you a coffee. Just don't get your hopes up."

Charlie gave Joe the finger and took a swig of his beer. "By the way, where's your brother?"

"Ryan? Him and Colton and Reese are on the way. Should be here soon."

"What's he gonna do?" asked Tim.

"He's staying on. Little bastard is built for it, likes it even. And after they promoted him to Lieutenant Colonel, Colton and Reese seem to enjoy being his lieutenants."

"Hope it doesn't go to his head."

"Too late, he had his chest puffed out a bit too far the other night and I had to pull rank on him. But he deserved it."

Tim reached for his lighter. He lit a cigar and grinned through a cloud of smoke. "Things went hard for him on the west side. Heard he caught a round to the chest."

"Yeah, he wore those bruises proudly. Luckily, he was wearing his vest."

Charlie glanced around the room. "Minus the radios, rifles, and occasional zombie, it does feel like old times. Kind of."

The conversation was broken up by the sound of Greg yelling, "Joe, radio on the private band. Come inside! Quickly!"

Joe jumped up and everyone followed him into the kitchen. Greg handed him the radio.

Joe said, "Go ahead."

A voice Joe didn't recognize came across the radio. "Reaper Two, this is Marine One. Permission to land in the back field?"

Joe was confused. The voice sounded familiar. "Marine One, Reaper Two, permission granted. Who am I speaking with?"

No response. Joe's back felt tight. Who did he just give permission to land? Joe waved his team to the garage and they grabbed their rifles and ran to the back field and took position. The rotors of a helicopter grew louder as it banked in off the bay and toward the house. Joe was trying to make out the copter when Tim yelled, "Isn't that Marine One? Holy shit."

Joe stood in silence until the chopper landed and shut down. Four marines rushed out followed by Cara, Ryan, Colton, Reese, Pat, Alex, the president, and the first lady.

Tim leaned over and whispered to Joe, "Guess you wouldn't have worn that old shirt and Carhartts if you knew the president was coming?"

The president was carrying a small cooler. Joe rushed out to meet him and stood at attention. He rendered a salute until the president returned it and put out his hand to shake. After a quick shake and a hug from the first lady, Joe asked, "Mister President?"

The president smiled. "Your daughter. She invited us while we were at the Coast Guard. She told me this was *the* party and we should be here."

Cara was blushing and had a big grin on her face.

"We would be honored to have you sit down and eat with us. I hope you like crabs."

The president looked at his wife. She nodded. "We would love to," said the president, "but first we need to see Matt Baylor."

Joe looked over his shoulder and saw Matt. The president waved Matt over and made introductions. "Son, I wanted to come personally thank you on behalf of a grateful nation for the sacrifices your brother made." One of the Marines handed the president a folded flag. The president handed Matt the flag and shook his hand. "Your family has our gratitude and the promise that his memory will live on along with his friend James."

Matt thanked the president and carried the flag to his trailer.

Joe led the president to one of the two picnic tables in his backyard. Pat and Alex sat next to Joe while the president sat across from him with his wife and Cara.

"Sir, I am curious." Joe said, "What's in the cooler?"

"It would have been rude not to bring something." The president handed Joe the cooler. "These are for you. Cara said it would make your day."

Inside the cooler sat two four packs of Innis & Gunn beer. Joe lifted one out, popped the cap on the table's edge, and handed it to the president. Joe popped one for himself and took a sip.

The president smiled. "Before we eat, would it be rude to talk business?"

"Sir, I had expected as much. Please, go ahead."

The president took a long sip of the beer. He stared at the bottle, saying, "Pretty good. And really hard to come by. How many of these will you be needing?"

"Mister President, I don't follow."

"What I mean is, how many of these will it take to convince you to help secure the White House and DC?"

Made in the USA
Middletown, DE
10 June 2020